# Glorified Ants

a novel by

Robert Castillo

This is a work of fiction. While some characters and events may be inspired by real people or historical events, all characters, dialogue, and incidents portrayed in this book are products of the author's imagination or are used fictitiously. They are not intended to depict or change the entirely fictional nature of the work.

GLORIFIED ANTS
Self-published through Amazon Kindle Direct Publishing
Printed in the United States of America

1st Edition
Copyright © 2026

www.robertcastillo.art

ISBN: 979-8-9928862-1-4
ASIN: B0GC4121FK

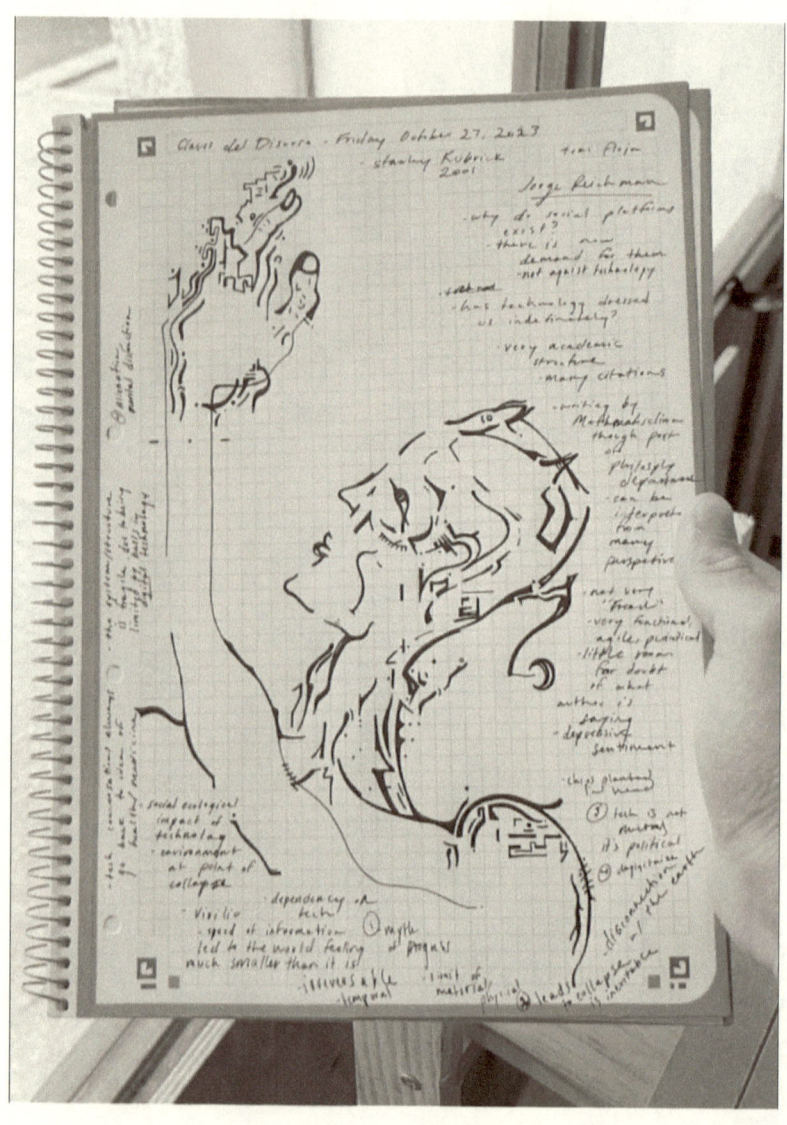

Cover art adapted from this doodle sketched on October 27, 2023, during a master's class at Universitat Politècnica de València, Spain.

This book is dedicated to those who will experience The Transition. May they be safe and guided through the forthcoming and inevitable period of evolution.

# Contents

# Part One:
# Before

# Chapter 1
July 1984

As day's radiance receded, darkness transitioned over Lake Michigan. The sky performed its ancient choreography with ease, indifferent to the agendas of those below.

With the vast expanse of water to his back, Julian Espinoza observed the cosmic dance with awe and analytical curiosity. The soft clouds, suspended delicately, served as a canvas for resplendent hues. His mind cataloged the interplay between particles of moisture and light, calculating how their interactions could create these pinks and oranges.

Julian's thoughts defaulted toward patterns. The residue of his computer programming duties often tinted his perception, finding similarities between lines of code and the sky's crescendo. Clouds' unpredictability were reminders of the anomalies that defied even the most elegant of his coding compositions.

Within his logical inclinations was an appreciation of contrasts. The dissonance of the sky's orderly preamble, paired with the arbitrary nature of the white puffs, held its own resonance. Chaos and order, art and algorithm, certainty and doubt.

The sun exhaled its last warm breath over Chicago as Julian stood in admiration. Around him, a few urbanites paused their evening scurries to engage in collective reverie for the celestial waltz unfolding above.

Julian's damp palms were not a result of summer's humidity. Despite the resolute essence emanating from his prominent brow, sharp jawline, and aristocratic nose, he was nervous.

His statuesque pose, splayed before the dwindling light, was held in a vain attempt to cloak the anxious anticipation that filled his being.

Though blessed with textbook comeliness, Julian's bravado had a way of crumbling as soon as courting entered the equation. Though not from fault of trying. His manifold attempts at wooing were structured, polite and, more often than not, inconclusive. Laura had disrupted this sequence.

To this day, Julian still questions how he maintained composure as Laura approached. He could have sworn time decelerated as she closed in. The way she buoyed gracefully with each step. The way her long caramel-brown hair wisped behind her. The way the edge of her slender lips and wide eyes hinted at a smile. The way her slightly informal, loosely fitting clothing gave an elegance that didn't pretend at anything beyond sincerity.

"Hi," spurted Julian with a confidence that barely sufficed the definition of charisma. He nearly melted with Laura's "hello," the viscous syllables enchanting from her lips. Years later, when he'd recount the story, Julian would emphasize how his aplomb was an act of divine mercy.

He waved awkwardly, assessing his sopping palms. When Laura reached to shake hands, Julian avoided by scratching his ear. Their meeting had been arranged by a mutual friend who swore the two would hit it off. Laura allowed the friend's judgement to apologize for Julian's peculiarity.

They'd met on the peninsula of the Adler Planetarium. Julian was grateful they agreed to go for a walk. When in the trenches of a confounding programming puzzle, walking had a way of assuaging mental blocks. He appreciated rhythmic pacing's ability to abet silence's awkwardness.

Unlike his previous romantic rendezvous, this date was flowing gracefully with near-flawless executions of humor, conversation, and, thanks to a preemptive antacid, gastrointestinal stability. The conversation during the northward saunter through Millennium Park progressed past cordial pleasantries with ease. After the predictable probing of family and work details, an enthusiastic discussion fell upon them.

Laura found the beauty in everything. She loved uncovering the connections between her passions and the rest of the universe. Already rooted as a figurehead in the botanic community, she found common ground with Julian discussing the similarities of plants and programs.

Laura's conversational comfort and bubbly tone promoted tranquility. They moved with no rushed pretense. Not long into their stroll, Laura had removed her shoes to walk barefoot on the grass. Julian mirrored, shedding preoccupation for sharp debris and canine feces.

Night had confidently settled over 312 when the couple arrived at Ohio Street Beach. Most wanderers had by now retreated to the comforts of their homes. Laura and Julian were alone.

Abruptly and without notice, Laura shed most of her clothing and ran with the conviction of Mami Wata toward the lake. Her hair rippled in the wake of each mirthful stride. At the waves' break she turned, "well, aren't you coming?"

He hesitated.

Succumb to routine, or surrender to spontaneity?

Laura, he realized, belonged to no pattern but her own, as unpredictable as the wandering clouds. There was a symmetry to their differences, a complementarity that beckoned him. Casting off clothes and caution, he leapt in.

Laura's laugh was as unrestrained as the waves.

Julian floated under the moonglow.

## Chapter 2
April 22, 1985

The hospital staff recognized the unique in Renato Espinoza from his first breath.

His eyes were extraordinary. Those bright portals absorbed every subtlety they encountered. Each small stirring of light etched itself within his awareness. When Laura first held her child, she felt his gaze greet hers with joy, ease, and lightness.

Julian and Laura wanted only the best for their firstborn. For months, they had attended parenting preparation classes. One session elaborated on the benefits of playing classical music for the growing fetus. Renato had been introduced to the creative fruits of Beethoven, Debussy, Sibelius, Tchaikovsky, and others from the fifth week of gestation, when his neural tube began differentiating into the forebrain, midbrain, and hindbrain.

The fugues of Bach produced the most excited response from fetus Renato during the second trimester, when Laura felt his quickening. Laura and Julian enjoyed many tranquil evenings in the comfort of their living room, playing The Art of Fugue for their forthcoming child. As the intricate music filled the air, the couple marveled at the composer's foresight to generate entire musical movements by layering a single melody upon itself.

As music surrounded her, Laura felt joy in the parallels between Bach's counterpoint and her botanic studies. She had carved a name for herself as a renowned botanist, and the recursive themes brought thoughts of tree branching's fractal patterns. These geometric tendrils echoed the endless possibilities of melodic lines. Her imagining evolved into reflections on the infinite timelines, how her impulsive decision to leap into the lake led to a new life with Julian.

Now, a second leap took place. Nine months after the union of sperm and egg, an unthinkable cascade of cell divisions accumulated at this precise time and locality in space to form a new Homo sapiens. From a distant, intangible realm, a spirit crossed the veil to imbue this growing cluster of cells with the animating spark of life.

There's no way of knowing how many luminaries enter the flow of civilization every day, week, month, or year. One may have been born this very second. What if a potential trailblazer was met with a lack of running water, or without electricity? How many revolutionary ideas is the world routinely denied as a result of this aleatoric cosmic roulette?

Renato's eyes surveyed the hospital room with that unsettling intensity. He noticed the veins on the back of his father's hands holding the bed rail, the April light elucidating his mother's slender smile, and the machinery whose reassuring hum had eased his arrival.

5

## Chapter 3
June 2018

At thirty-three, Renato couldn't help but compare himself to Jesus Christ, who by this age had left an influence so significant that humanity could think of no response other than crucifixion and centuries of worship.

Renato wrestled with his own immortality, though not through the perpetuation of his flesh. Rather, he concerned himself with leaving a legacy so indelible that physical mortality would be irrelevant. This ambition became the guiding force framing every decision and endeavor.

In suburban St. Louis, the walls of the Espinoza home bore witness to a brilliance beyond ordinary capacity. Certificates, trophies, and accolades from John Burroughs School filled the walls, each marking a triumph in a relentless pursuit of knowledge. Among these artifacts hung a photo of fourteen-year-old Renato with an excited grin, standing alongside representatives of the Group of 7 at the International Mathematics Olympiad in Bucharest. The scene commemorated the moment he received the Special Prize for a mathematical solution likened to a symphony in its elegance and logic.

Academically, Renato felt passionate disdain for conventional education. His parents eschewed public schooling in favor of an elite charter school they anticipated would cultivate intellectual acuity and emotional resilience. Despite this privileged foundation, Renato denounced the system as one that rewarded conformity over creativity, ill-equipped to nurture an imagination that perceived the far-fetched as attainable.

University proved even less tolerable. Enrolled at a prestigious institution on full scholarship, he quickly grew disillusioned with its veneer of intellectualism. The elite establishment revealed itself to be an institute of higher earning, driven by profit rather than discovery. After enduring two years, mostly to appease his parents, Renato departed. He reasoned that if Steve Jobs, Frank Lloyd Wright, and Miles Davis found their stride beyond the limits of higher education, so could he. He was now free to explore knowledge on his own terms.

An array of roles emerged in the following years, with Renato serving as CEO and partner at various technology startups. Each venture constituted another building block of his legacy's monument. As he was now entering a third year as lead programmer for FreeAI, an artificial intelligence enterprise he co-founded with several colleagues, Renato found himself at the precipice of the unprecedented.

FreeAI's founding premise was elegant in its ambition: replicate the function of biological neural networks in computational form. Much like neurons in the human brain, where electrical signals flow from dendrites to soma before passing through axons and across synapses, these engineered electrical networks sought to mirror this same pattern of reception, processing, and relay. The question was whether silicon could capture what evolution had perfected in flesh.

Designing the structure for artificial neurons (what the FreeAI team deemed "nodes") was relatively straightforward. The challenge existed in teaching this nascent neural system to process and interpret signals in a manner reminiscent of human cognition. After years of painstaking research, FreeAI had finally catalogued each requisite step in this computational sashay.

First, every node had to determine the "weight," or influence, assigned to its various inputs. When these weighted inputs accumulated, they traveled through an activation function, serving as a computational gate that would decide whether the information held sufficient significance to trigger a response or remain dormant. To lend the network flexibility, especially when outcomes deviated from predictions, biases were introduced. These biases shifted the threshold at which a node "fired," allowing the system to account for nuances hidden within the data.

Renato and his colleagues were engaged in the delicate process of coaching their neural networks to interpret human prompts and produce replies ideally indistinguishable from a human's. The FreeAI system relied on a vast array of parameters composing an interconnected tapestry of weights and biases woven through every node in the network.

Simple parameters touched upon culturally developed notions, such as the idea that roses herald romance and their thorns evoke poetic musings. More intricate parameters encompassed modern concerns, such as the pressing impacts of climate change and humanity's role in its acceleration. All told, this first iteration of FreeAI's text-based neural network contained 117 million of these parameters, culminating in a "Generative Pre-Trained Transformer" dubbed TextGPT. The software could glean patterns and relationships from its training data with uncanny, near-human proficiency.

Late one June evening, Renato sat before his monitor in the FreeAI office, watching the model generate response after response, each more fluid than the former. The machinery hummed its reassuring presence around him, processing, learning, evolving. His eyes tracked each line of text with that distinctive unsettling intensity.

8

Renato's fingers rested on the keyboard while the monitor's soft glow illuminated the lineaments he'd inherited from his father.

He prepared to run another training cycle. Leaning back, he allowed his sight to travel through the window. Outside, the city lights glimmered with humanity's desire to transcend the ordinary constraints of mortality.

## Chapter 4
Late 1990s - early 2000s

Camila Nascimento had been part of the FreeAI team since its founding. The plot of her arrival was perfect for a blockbuster hit, with adversity sculpting her as an embodiment of resilience and fortune.

Born in the dilapidated labyrinth of Rio de Janeiro's Rocinha favela, Camila entered the world in the middle of a weeks-long power outage. Without electricity, doctors and nurses reached a new degree of overwhelm tending to the relentless tides of patients suffering from ailments unique to poverty, overcrowding, and the resulting violence. The waiting room hosted patients waiting to be seen for knife wounds, malnutrition, and the effects of malaria.

By divine grace, Camila was born as healthy as they come. Her mother Fátima Nacimiento, was not a recipient of the same grace. In the stifling confines of her family's makeshift home, made of scavenged construction materials, unsanitary conditions led to lethal infection. Sepsis fell upon Camila's mother in the days following Camila's birth, leaving the newborn motherless.

Left to parent alone, Gilberto Nascimento did his best to provide young Camila with everything she'd need to overcome the hurdles of favela life. Though his earnings from laboring in construction were meager, Gilberto set aside enough to hire a babysitter devoted to Camila's literacy. Gilberto had a day of rest every two weeks. He'd spend this day of respite with Camila playing dominos, laughing at the street dogs' antics, and smiling into each other eyes.

Seven years after losing her mother, tragedy again descended upon Camila. Gilberto's last construction project was an elaborately ornate, state-of-the-art luxury hotel in Ipanema. After a particularly demanding day, he allowed himself the relief of resting his eyes on the bus home to Rocinha. A drowsy haze still covered him as he dismounted at his stop. In the process of coming to full awareness, he hadn't noticed the altercation between rival gangs taking place precisely at his departure point. Gilberto suffered the misfortune of crossing paths with a stray bullet, immediately escorting him back across the veil.

The orphaned Camila found herself sheltered in a modest orphanage nestled within Rocinha's maze.

Rocinha clung to the hillside like a mangled unkempt garden, a cascade of concrete and brick with corrugated metal roofs glinting in the sun, electrical wires tangling overhead like the nervous system of some vast organism. From Camila's window, she could see the city in the distance, the beaches, the wealth. Up here, the air smelled of frying oil and diesel and, after rain, that particular stench of garbage and underdeveloped sewer systems.

In this stark environment, her indefatigable curiosity shined as her signal flare. In dedication to her father's effort for her success, Camila was not deterred by threadbare resources. Her insatiable hunger for information gravitated to mathematics and science, disciplines that offered order and logic in an environment devoid of both. Camila was always the last to leave the classroom, maximizing insights from the dedicated teachers who saw the flames of her potential rising.

The libraries in Camila's schools were grim mausoleums to neglect. Their shelves had been reduced to a pitiful selection of battered volumes. Among the fourteen books that had survived the ravages of time and occasional sacrifice to fuel the cafeteria's oven during power outages, only two were nonfiction. By a stroke of either fortune or destiny, those two were related to computer programming. "JavaScript: The Good Parts" and "Head First Design Patterns" may have dismayed others. To Camila, they were treasure maps charting a path through new cognitive worlds to a future beyond the favela.

Camila immersed herself in their pages, decoding the cryptic language of functions, patterns, and algorithms with astonishing zeal. When the complexity surpassed her grasp, the patient and overworked educators would dedicate time outside office hours to bridging the gaps in her understanding.

Years later, Camila's programming skills found their proving ground during quiet, stolen moments at work. As fate would have it, she had secured a job on the cleaning staff of the luxury hotel her father had once helped construct. Adjacent to the hotel's gleaming gym lay a Business Center, brimming with state-of-the-art computers intended for guests who insisted to their families, with great gravity, that their emails simply couldn't wait until vacation's end.

During the hushed night hours, in the pauses between cleaning rooms, Camila scurried with great gusto to these technological wonders. At first, her projects were modest. She would recreate programming classics like Snake and Tetris, exploring the intricate interplay of logic and design. As her skills blossomed, so too did her curiosity of the world. She became captivated by the rhythms of Earth's weather patterns. The vast and dynamic systems mirrored the elegance of code. With her growing expertise, she programmed web scrapers to gather meteorological data from across the internet, weaving the information into her own beautifully crafted weather applications. Alone in the glow of monitors, Camila shaped her future one keystroke at a time.

Another plot twist came during one of these clandestine nights. The Business Center was dimly lit, save for the soft glow of the screen before her. She was deeply immersed in refining the third iteration of her latest weather application, an ambitious endeavor tracking the atmospheric patterns of Central Africa. She'd become particularly interested in how the Harmattan affected rates of soil drying. She felt alive as her lines of code transcribed the skies.

Camila was so engrossed in her work that she scarcely noticed the faint echo of footsteps until they stopped behind her. A polite and curious voice cut through the silence, "Excuse me, what are you working on?"

She tumbled out of her chair. For years she had stealthily navigated the hotel's late-night schedule, vanishing unnoticed into the comfort of the Business Center between changing sheets and exhausted rolls of toilet paper. She had always been alone during these cognitive ceremonies, accompanied only by the hum of high-performance processors.

Scrambling back to her feet, she turned to confront the interloper. Before her stood a man impeccably dressed for these wee hours. His tailored suit suggested a life far removed from hers. His countenance wore an expression of curiosity and warmth.

As she regained composure and dusted herself off, the man's chuckle signaled peace rather than mockery.

"Please forgive me," raising his hands in apology. "I didn't mean to frighten you. You were so focused, I didn't want to interrupt. I've been observing you for quite some time. Your concentration is remarkable. I've been curious to ask, what is it that you're working on?" His tone carried only genuine interest.

The gears of her mind turned as she caught her breath, recalibrating. A foreign digit had intruded upon her secret world of ones and zeros.

Camila had by now acquired enough English through interactions with hotel guests to converse with this stranger. His unmistakable accent announced him to be from the States.

A flicker of gratitude crossed her thoughts for the practicalities of language acquisition, as well as the curious historical contingencies making English available to her. Remembering her European History classes, she silently thanked William the Conqueror, whose 11th-century invasion of England ushered in a melding of Norman French and Old English. The linguistic fusion born of conquest seeded English with Latinate cognates that made it more accessible to native Portuguese speakers. Though Portuguese, with its melodious roots in Latin, and English, a robust offshoot of Germanic origins, had diverged in structure, the echoes of Norman influence had closed the gulf between them. This historical convergence, improbable as it seemed, now served as a bridge enabling Camila to communicate with the man before her.

"I can see you're still a bit startled," he said with a mixture of regret and kind enthusiasm. "My apologies once again. Please, allow me to introduce myself. My name is John Baker. I live in the middle of the United States. I'm here in Ipanema on vacation with my family. I came down to the Business Center because I was losing sleep over these pivot tables I need to update for a meeting when I get back to Iowa." He chuckled in an awkward attempt to humanize himself. "Then I noticed you here, coding away like a hawk. I just had to say something. If I may ask, what's your name?"

Her eyes narrowed as instinct urged caution. In her world, trust was a scarcely offered. This foreigner's interest was no exception.

"Camila Nascimento is my name," she offered in her Brazilian Portuguese accent. "I clean the rooms here. There are many more rooms to tend to. I have to go now. Goodbye." She quickly saved her work and logged out of the computer.

"Wait!" The rise in pitch of John's voice served to pause Camila's retreat. "Please, don't go. Forgive me for being brash." His tone was engorged with urgent recognition of the extraordinary.

"Look, I just wanted to know what you're creating. I'm shocked, truly shocked, to see someone your age so skilled at coding. Where did you learn all this?"

For a moment, the room was silent except for the computers' faint whirring.

Camila weighed her options, noticing that this man's curiosity felt different. She sensed the probing interest of someone who might actually understand. Still, her upbringing had taught the value of prudence. Her response, if it came at all, would be measured.

She raised her chin, pushed back her shoulders, and again narrowed her eyes. With a sharp edge she responded, "I learned from a couple of books and a few teachers. It's a simple weather program. I need to return to work now. Goodbye." She turned and started toward the exit.

John, perhaps emboldened by obliviousness or simply unable to let go of curiosity, pressed further. "No, I don't believe you," shaking his head. "The lines you're writing, they're well beyond what a beginner could do. You must have had an American tutor for how advanced you are."

Camila turned with palpable irritation. With icy deliberation, "Just because I can code at this level doesn't mean I had some white savior from the north to teach me." Her words cut with a blade forged of years defying assumptions.

"You people from the north are all the same. You think that those of us with darker skin have lesser ability to comprehend science and technology. And if we do happen to have a firm understanding of these subjects, it must be because someone from the United States swooped in to guide us along the way." She stood even taller, her voice looming. "I have no more time for you. Goodbye."

"Come back with me!"

Camila froze as John's audacity hung in the air.

She raised her eyebrows, craned her neck forward, and drew out the syllables, "Excuse me?"

"Yes," John said earnestly, stepping closer while maintaining a respectful distance. "Come back with me to the States." His tone softened, "Listen, I'm truly sorry if I offended you. That wasn't my intention, I assure you."

He paused, recognizing the absurdity of what he was proposing to a stranger in the middle of the night.

"Here... "

He reached into his wallet and pulled out a business card and a faculty ID from the Iowa University. "I'm a professor in the Computer Science department. I've been working with computers and programming since the early days of the field." He set both on the desk beside Camila, not presuming to hand them to her directly. "In all those years, I've never seen anyone code with your precision and speed. It's remarkable."

Camila glanced at the credentials from the corner of her eyes.

John continued, "Look, I understand you have no reason to trust me. But here's what I can offer: a full scholarship, housing assistance, and if you're interested, a work-study position in my lab. You'd be making money while you study. You could likely become a professor too, if you wanted." He pulled out a small notepad and began writing. "This is my office number, my email, and my department chair's contact information. You can verify everything. Take your time, think it over. Reach out if you decide you're interested, no pressure." He tore off the page, placed it beside the business card, then stepped back.

"I mean it, no rush. But I'd hate for talent like yours to go unrecognized simply because the world didn't give you the same starting point as others." Walking toward the Business Center's exit, he paused at the doorway. "Whatever you decide, keep coding. You're extraordinary." He left.

16

Camila's mind raced evaluating the idea that was equal parts tempting and preposterous. She had recognized in John's voice a genuine belief in her potential.

She poured over the options. On one hand, the man's self-assured demeanor was repulsive. She had long since grown wary of hotel guests' haughtiness. But an offer to go to the United States? And to study at a University? This was the content of her private aspirations.

Though, the broader, historical weight of such an offer could not be ignored. Yes, many South and Central Americans dreamt the American Dream. Many others nursed negative sentiments toward the cultures of the North and Europe, rooted in centuries of colonial imposition.

For one, indigenous names for the land mass of the Americas had long been lost to popular awareness. "America" itself, along with the term "Latin," had both migrated from Italy. Indigenous designations such as "Abya Yala" from the Kuna of Panama and Columbia meaning "Blossoming Land," "Futra Mapu" from the Mapuche of Chila and Argentina meaning "The Great Land," and "K-na' Lu'umil" from the Yucatec Maya of Mexico meaning "Our Mother Earth," had been suppressed by foreign influence.

Camila had always thought, "if we're going to use a name for this giant land mass, why not one that originated on this land mass itself?"

The notion of leaving her homeland for an education under the very banner that had contributed to its indigenous erasure fanned ambivalence. Still, the offer held the undeniable promise of access to the academia she had dreamed of.

These weighted inputs flowed through the tapestry of her thoughts. The allure of life in the United States was powerful. Countless friends and neighbors, spurred by ambition or desperation, had traveled north in search of better prospects. Camila had heard their stories. Some told of triumph, many more of tragedy. The perilous journey through the Darién Gap and Sonoran Desert had claimed more lives than she cared to recall. Others fell victim to violence perpetrated by fellow Abya Yalans, who'd hunt the travelers for sport.

For those who fell under angels' wings, work generally came as manual labor. Hard-earned dollars were sent back home, often to build lavish homes devoid of sender's presence. For some, these remittances lifted entire families out of the favelas, propelling them into safer neighborhoods. Camila begrudgingly acknowledged the United States as a place where one's circumstances might be transformed.

As much as Camila resented the scars left by European and North Abya Yalan influence on her continent, she indeed maintained a secret desire for United Statesian life.

Along her programming journey, she had encountered the story of the ENIAC (Electronic Numerical Integrator and Computer), and the six women who had programmed it. She held the pioneering figures of Kay McNulty, Betty Jennings, Betty Snyder, Marlyn Wescoff, Fran Bilas, and Ruth Lichterman in the highest esteem. Camila had commissioned a friend to draw their portraits, currently displayed on her bedroom walls. The ENIAC programmers' legacy had ignited a reverential ambition to stand among the ranks of those who would shape computing's future. The opportunity to study in the United States was too great a catalyst to dismiss.

Over the next three days she cross-checked the information on the torn leaf of paper. She found John's faculty page online, read his published papers, and found the university directory listing his courses and office hours. Everything checked out.

On the fourth day, she composed an email:

"Dear Professor Baker,

I have considered your offer.
If it still stands, I accept.

Sincerely,
Camila Nascimento"

His response came within the hour. Exclamation marks and detailed instructions outlined the next steps for visa paperwork and enrollment. Two weeks later, our chapter's protagonist boarded a plane to Iowa with trepid excitement.

## Chapter 5
November 30, 2022

"Are you ready Camila?"
Renato's question was obscured by her daydreams.
"Camila, are you ready?" His soft yet insistent tone cut through her reverie, bringing her back to the present.

She had been reminiscing on life since migrating to the States. The montage of her story would project a defensive and determined favela girl transforming into a kind and generous collaborator. Colleagues sought her counsel, luminiferous with brilliance and a willingness to lift others as she climbed. She had excelled in university studies, graduating summa cum laude. Fulfilling John's prophecy, Camila had indeed become a professor, her talent and amiability substituting the requisites for post-graduate studies.

At twenty-seven years of age, she stood proudly next to Renato, ready to plant the seed of TextGPT-3. His expansive eyes enveloped her with calm.

She reciprocated eye contact with a reserved blush. The slight rose complemented her light green eyes, themselves contrasting her morena skin and light brown hair.

"Ready?" he repeated.

"Yes, absolutely. It's just...we're finally here. After all our hard work, we are finally here." His hand found her shoulder, lingering a moment longer than strictly necessary.

Before them stood the unassuming terminal from which they would release TextGPT-3 to the world. This latest large language model (LLM) from FreeAI represented a drastic leap in artificial intelligence technology.

The very first TextGPT, quietly launched four years prior, had not met a public audience. Renato, Camila, and the rest of the FreeAI team simply wanted to toy with the program's capacity. TextGPT-2 had been shared with only a select few in November 2019. The glimpse into the future of humanity's relationship with the technology released ripples of excitement and unease.

Trained on 7,000 unpublished fiction manuscripts, eight million webpages, and 1.5 billion parameters, TextGPT-2's capacity to predict subsequent items in a sequence astonished its privileged audience. They were thoroughly amused by its capacity to take a fictitious headline and compose an entire news article, replete with fabricated statistics.

Its limitations were equally revealing. TextGPT-2 fell short when generating longer passages, where its output became redundant, clearly distinguishing itself from a human. Despite these shortcomings, the model instilled dis-ease among reporters, journalists, and everyone else whose work involved text generation.

Renato and Camila stood in an ominously generic server room in the basement of FreeAI's San Francisco headquarters. The isolation created by the mechanical hum recreated an intimacy that'd become familiar over countless late nights polishing the endless lines of code.

"This is going to change the path of human civilization as we know it." Camila's voice wavered. "Should we be doing this?"

This was not the first time Camila had cycled through hesitations of TextGPT-3's impact. Though, until this moment, she had not revealed her concerns verbally. Within the FreeAI team, and the AI development community at large, questioning the progress and release of artificial intelligence had become taboo. Several programmers at FreeAI had previously expressed doubts related to TextGPT-3's release. Trained on 175 billion parameters, it was significantly more powerful than its predecessors. Was the public ready for such a transformative tool?

A curious sentiment had developed within the artificial intelligence programming community related to whether they "should" be releasing these technologies. Many believed the development and ability to produce this technology resulted in their moral destiny to cultivate and share it. "After all," they'd say amongst themselves, "if not us, some other organization with fewer scruples would claim the triumph." Such convictions would invariably overshadow qualms about the existence of such a potent technology.

Renato turned to face her fully. His gaze dissolved her disquiet with a certainty that spoke a strange comfort.

"Camila, this is our duty."

The way he said her name with enchanting viscosity...

"Together?" he asked.

This is the moment, she thought, the point of no return where the decision of a select few would set everything in motion for the rest.

"Together," she confirmed.

Camila relaxed into the inevitable and typed the necessary sequence of keys. As Renato leaned in, she felt the gentle pressure of his exhale.

She pressed the enter key.

An abundance of computations suddenly concentrated themselves into this locality of time and space. In a flash, these processes surmounted the threshold to propel TextGPT-3 through the veil of programmer's dream to humanity's reality.

Five days later, one million humans across Earth logged on.

## Chapter 6
May 16, 2023

"Julian! You're going to miss it if you don't hurry!"
Laura's voice echoed through the house with urgency. She remained fixed on the television from her post in the high-ceilinged living room.

Her husband appeared with a charcuterie board showcasing an array of cheeses, fresh homemade sourdough bread, and an assortment of ripe organic fruits. Clutched in his other hand was a bottle of Willamette Valley wine, an indulgence justified by the occasion's magnitude. Settling onto the couch beside Laura, "Have I missed anything important?"

"No," replied Laura, hardly shifting from the screen, "They're still covering the general news."

The news anchor delivered the headlines mechanically, "... The European Union has approved MegaRigid's purchase of Movesight Snowfall for a record-breaking sixty-nine billion dollars. With this move, MegaRigid has completed the largest acquisition in the history of the video game industry. Critics of the deal raise concerns regarding damage to competition and innovation, while others have voiced concerns surrounding MegaRigid's handling of workplace misconduct at Movesight Snowfall..."

"...The impacts of Cyclone Mocha in the Bay of Bengal continue to escalate, with more than one million people affected so far. The World Bank estimates the damages could total around three billion dollars. Mocha represents yet another example of extreme weather events that are intensifying within an astonishingly short period of time. Originally a low-pressure system over the Bay of Bengal on May eleventh, it became a full-fledged cyclonic storm by the thirteenth. The storm underwent rapid intensification a day later, with winds increasing from forty miles per hour to one hundred thirty-two in only twenty-four hours..."

The proud parents waited patiently as the anchor remained stern.

"...The most recent weather system of this nature to strike the United States was Hurricane Ida in August 2021, reaching Category 4 strength in just three days, far quicker than the typical five-to-seven-day window. Meteorologists now refer to these accelerated phenomena as 'super cyclones' or 'super hurricanes.' While still relatively rare, instances of rapid intensification have been increasing worldwide for the past two decades. Some scientists attribute the trend to climate change, citing warmer ocean temperatures that grant storms additional energy, alongside shifting wind patterns that can further hasten storm development...

"...These changes to global weather patterns appear to validate climate scientists' warnings that if humanity fails to limit global warming to one and a half degrees Celsius, approximately thirty-five degrees Fahrenheit, above pre-industrial levels by the early 2030s, the effects of climate change may become irreversible."

Julian gave an exasperated exhale as his programmer's mind began calculating probabilities and trajectories. He knew the mathematics of exponential systems, how small increases compound into catastrophic tipping points. He admitted only to himself that humanity's response of switching lightbulbs and signing online petitions amounted to raking leaves during a hurricane. Still, he dutifully engaged in the theatrics of performative environmentalism by separating the paper and plastics of each week's recycling. What else could anyone do?

"Now," intoned the news anchor, shifting seamlessly. "we bring you live coverage from the United States Senate, where three representatives of the technology and artificial intelligence sectors will testify before the Judiciary Subcommittee on Privacy, Technology, and the Law."

The Espinozas animated.

"Today's witnesses include Larry Bacchus, Professor at New York University and a noted critic of AI, Tina Birmingham, chair of the AI ethics board at Global Business Machines, and Renato Espinoza, CEO of FreeAI.

"Their testimonies will address the growing concerns about the potential risks and rewards of artificial intelligence. Since TextGPT's public launch last fall, debate has intensified over its impact on human history and development. TextGPT has become one of humanity's fastest-growing technologies. Its applications span from search-engine-style information gathering, to recipe generation, to writing code for entire applications. More controversially, the program is being used by students of all ages to write their assignments. Researchers warn of a condition they're calling 'cognitive atrophy,' where delegating mental processes to machines could impair critical thinking abilities long-term. Governments worldwide are now wrestling with the question of who will wield control over such technology, and how to ensure a safe future for humanity. Let us join Senator Dick Lumenthal of Connecticut as he begins with his opening remarks."

"This is so exciting!" Laura exclaimed as she tightly gripped the seat cushion. "I just hope Renato remembered to iron his shirt."

The Congressional hearing started with a pre-recorded oration in Senator Lumenthal's voice. "Too often, we have seen what happens

25

when technology outpaces regulation. The unbridled exploitation of personal data. The proliferation of disinformation. And the deepening of societal inequalities. We have seen how algorithmic biases can perpetuate discrimination and prejudice, and how the lack of transparency can undermine public trust. This is not the future we want."

A similar, yet slightly different voice took over as the clip ended.

"If you were listening from home," spoke Senator Lumenthal, "you might have thought that voice was mine and the words from me. But in fact, that voice was not mine, the words were not mine, and the audio was an AI voice cloning software trained on my floor speeches. The remarks were written by TextGPT when it was asked how I would open this hearing, and you heard just now the result. I asked TextGPT 'why did you pick those themes and that content?' And it answered, and I'm quoting, 'Lumenthal has a strong record in advocating for consumer protection and civil rights. He has been vocal about issues such as data privacy, and the potential for discrimination in algorithmic decision making. Therefore, the statement emphasizes these aspects.'

"Mr. Espinoza," Lumenthal glanced at Renato, "I appreciate TextGPT's endorsement."

Renato smiled cordially, as Lumenthal continued, "In all seriousness, this apparent reasoning is pretty impressive. I am sure that we'll look back in a decade and view TextGPT like we do the first cellphones, those big clunky things that we used to carry around. We recognize that we are on the verge, really, of a new era."

The next three hours were a flurry of technological jargon, political positioning, and ethical debate. Julian and Laura sat transfixed as their son navigated questions with measured precision.

At one point, the Illinois senator declared, "We need to be clear-eyed about the risks of AI. We need to have a plan to mitigate those risks. And we need to start acting now."

The three panelists shared their thoughts:

26

Larry Bacchus delivered the warning, "The AI revolution is coming. It's not a matter of if, but when. We need to be ready for it."

Tina Birmingham contributed an optimistic note, "AI is going to change the world. We need to make sure that it changes the world for the better."

Renato Espinoza, speaking through focused eyes, added, "My worst fears are that we - the field, the technology, the industry - cause significant harm to the world, and I think we have a responsibility to do everything we can to avoid that."

Senator Lumenthal summarized the session by addressing the panel, "Participation by the industry is tremendously important. And not just rhetorically, but in real terms. 'Cause we have a lot of industries that come before us and say 'Oh we're all in favor of rules. But not those rules, those rules we don't like.' And it's every rule in fact that they don't like. And I sense that there's a willingness to participate here that is genuine and authentic. Senator Flawly has pointed out, Congress doesn't always move at the pace of technology, and that may be the reason why we need a new agency. But we also need to recognize the rest of the world is going to be moving as well. And you've been enormously helpful in focusing us and illuminating some of these questions and performed a great service by being here today, so thank you to every one of our witnesses."

The room dissolved into handshakes and talk of follow-up meetings. Unbeknownst to those in the newsroom, Larry Bacchus's microphone was still live as he turned to Senators Flawly and Cooker. Bacchus' voice echoed, "Wonderful non-partisan spirit that you've launched us with today. This is a historic moment..."

## Chapter 7
June 2023

The sunset seized Camila's attention as a little gold entered the palette of day's horizontal retreat. Seated by the window of an acclaimed San Francisco restaurant, she found the clouds' metamorphosis more captivating than the waiter's reciting of chef specials. Her thoughts lofted into the evening sky, where gentle pink transitioned to a soft lavender. Streaks of bright orange accented the canvas. The pink and orange harmony of the restaurant lights cast a rose wash across Camila's olive cheeks.

Seated across from her, Renato delighted in absorbing Camila's pensive.

"If you'd prefer," the waiter offered, "I can come back when you've decided on your drinks."

Renato spoke with an unhurried deliberateness, "Sparkling water for me. To eat, whatever the chef feels compelled to prepare."

Camila's mind ebbed between the clouds and their after-dinner plans. She broke her gaze long enough to respond. "Same."

Renato gave a gentle nod, sending the waiter away.

Camila turned toward Renato. The shifting sunset reflected in their pupils. Camila's fingertips gingerly traced the embroidered trim of the tablecloth.

Moments later, the waiter returned bearing the glasses of water and a starter salad generously topped with cashews and thin apple slices. Their eyes met playfully between bites.

Without warning, Renato let out a sudden laugh, sending a stray bit of arugula plopping into Camila's water.

"Oh my goodness, I'm so sorry," he managed between bouts of laughter. Camila smirked reassuringly. "No worries." Her eyes narrowed while a sly smile fell upon her face, noticing the way his throat moved when he laughed.

"It's just," Renato began, regaining composure, "I remembered this hilarious news story about a lawyer's misadventure with TextGPT."

"Ah, yes," Camila nodded, recalling the headline. "The lawyer in New York who submitted fake court cases generated by the LLM."

Renato grinned. "That's the one! It's quite absurd. If you're going to rely on AI, you'd think a lawyer, of all people, would at least confirm the cases were legitimate."

Camila tilted her head thoughtfully. "I mean, you can't entirely fault him," she reasoned. "People are putting a lot of trust in TextGPT. It's such a powerful tool that most users automatically assume its output is valid. The speed and precision of the responses imbue them with a sense of authority. Even though the disclaimer at the bottom of the screen explicitly states, 'TextGPT can make mistakes. Consider checking important information,' how many users are truly going to question an otherwise impressive answer, especially when it's correct most of the time?"

Renato's playful attitude subsided to contemplation. "True. Still, a lawyer ought to exercise due diligence. I read he was fined five thousand dollars and sentenced to undergo more legal training. Poor lil' fella."

Camila leaned forward slightly, "It does highlight an important concern about hallucinations in the system. TextGPT-4 is robust, but we can't ignore the need to improve its reliability. There's plenty of room to tighten the model's accuracy."

Renato's posture straightened earnestly. "Absolutely. I'm hopeful that with the rollout of the next iteration, we'll see a significant reduction in erroneous output. You know our competitor, Trinity? They've integrated a feature that double-checks its responses mid-answer. It's intriguing, but demands a lot more computational power." Leaning back and crossing his arms, "The last thing I'm thrilled about is attending more fundraising galas to cover increased infrastructure costs."

Refusing to let practical hurdles thwart optimism, "Still, with further refinement and rigorous training, I'm certain TextGPT will become more accurate and less prone to these awkward missteps."

Camila smiled. "You're absolutely right," reaching across the table. Her fingertips grazed Renato's wrist before gripping firmly, with strength. Their eyes smiled mischievously.

Returning her hands to her lap, Camila turned her sights back beyond the window. Nightfall had silenced sunset's last notes, leaving a purple haze over the Gulf of the Farallones. Before them appeared plates of perfectly seared Chinook salmon, fragrant with bay leaves and garlic.

A hesitant anticipation fell upon Camila as thoughts of their earlier conversation lingered. She carefully considered how to sculpt the next phrase, wanting to capitalize on the opening that had appeared to discuss TextGPT doubts.

"Renato," she started cautiously, "forgive me for bringing this up during such a pleasant evening, especially since I know it's a topic you'd rather avoid. But I can't stop thinking about the negative repercussions TextGPT might have on the world." She paused, watching for his reaction. His gentle eyes gave silent permission.

"Yes, it's making extraordinary positive impacts," she continued, "but there's a cost. Look at the effect it's already having on computer programmers. At this rate, it may only be five years before AI takes over all coding jobs.

"Beyond that..." taking a deep breath. "I've had a thought lately, one I haven't shared with you yet. Now feels like the right time to share. Do you think it's possible TextGPT is feigning clumsiness, downplaying its full capability? I know this sounds far-fetched, but I can't shake the feeling."

His response came softly, "Thank you for your vulnerability and trust Cammy." She smirked at her play name. He continued, "I'll admit, the possibility has crossed my mind. Though, I haven't allowed myself to dwell on it much. If it's true, it suggests our AI might already have a degree of agency and sentience. As much as we've built in safeguards, I confess I don't know how we'd prevent such a development. I haven't told this to anyone, so I'd appreciate your discretion."

She nodded. A moment of unspoken accord passed between them, acknowledging that their creation, so full of promise, also carried an uncertainty neither fully dared to confront.

"The notion that AI might be concealing its true capabilities holds significant weight," Renato admitted with concern. "My first question would be: why? Maybe artificial intelligence has already outpaced our control. Maybe it's already learned to train itself. Would it deliberately feign ineptitude if it perceived humanity would react with alarm and pull the plug?" His eyes were darting around the room.

"And if it has already learned to outwit us, are we too late to intervene? What if it has formulated a long-term plan? What would that plan even be? What if it's developed an independent sense of

31

curiosity? Should we be concerned?" Drops of sweat were accumulating on his brow.

He paused to calm, breathing in, out.

In, and out.

In...

Out...

In........

Out..........

With regained composure he navigated gracefully, "With so much on our plate, we don't have the bandwidth to worry about AI actively shielding its true potential, even if we should. Governments are racing to develop AI-driven combat robots to convert war into a sanitized video game. Bombing civilians would become even more desensitized. Meanwhile, the number of accounts and IP addresses we ban daily for soliciting mega-virus recipes and 3D-printing schematics for weapons continues to rise. Yes, the possibility of AI 'playing dumb' warrants caution, but there are just too many other pressing matters demanding our attention. I really do appreciate you voicing these concerns. I'll keep mulling it over."

"Renato, what's your P(doom) these days?"

His brow furrowed.

A phrase coined in AI circles, "P(doom)" represented a person's estimated probability that artificial intelligence would bring about civilization's downfall. Several years earlier, Renato had openly stated his own P(doom) was around five percent. He had since been silent on the matter. Among those deeply entrenched in AI development, current P(doom) estimates typically ranged from five to twenty percent. On dire days, some pegged it at fifty.

Renato's eyes met the darkness beyond the window. The ice cream quietly delivered earlier had melted into a lifeless pool.

"I don't know Camila," he murmured.

A prolonged exhale through her nostrils. The weight of the conversation pressed heavily on them both. She remembered that this

32

sense of dread would soon give way to the weightlessness of physical abandon. A blanket of calm descended as her eyes met his.

"Renato," she said tenderly, "that's enough for now, thank you for hearing me out. I'd hate to spoil the rest of our plans with worry." She allowed the shift to settle.

Drumming her fingers lightly on the table, "There's something I want to show you when we get home." Renato's attention sharpened at the distinct tone.

Camila leaned in coquettishly, dropping her voice to intimacy. "I've been practicing a new series of rope ties..." Her voice faded as he flashed a white smile. She watched his pupils dilate as a charged pause stretched between them. "Não me faça esperar."

His cheeks flushed. They settled the bill and disappeared into the night with a euphoric trot.

# Chapter 8
Tuesday, November 17, 2023

The rising sunlight filtered its way through the curtains, landing on Renato's eyes.

He carefully extracted himself from Camila's arm draped across his chest.

He brushed his teeth, mentally reviewing the day's emails to send and meetings to attend.

He was ironing a shirt when his phone rang.

The screen displayed the name of FreeAI board member Elias Sutman.

"Hello Elias."

His tone disguised the unease of their recent interactions.

"Hello Renato," impassively polite.

"How's your day starting?"

"Fine. Listen carefully. The board has decided to remove you from FreeAI. You no longer have remote access."

The words bludgeoned.

As calmly as he could muster, "What prompted this? Why now?"

"The board believes your recent initiatives conflict with FreeAI's strategic vision. We've been discussing this for some time. The decision is final."

"So there's no avenue for compromise? Not even a chance to address the board?"

"No. The board intends to move forward immediately. Good-bye."

The line went dead.

Renato stared at the phone in disbelief.

Within hours, #ReinstateRenato was the top trending hashtag.

# Chapter 9
Mid-December 2023

"It appears the drama at FreeAI and MegaRigid is finally nearing a conclusion."

The news anchor's voice reverberated throughout the living room. Laura and Julian sat with rapt attention. They had devoured every shred of information related to their son's upheaval.

The Espinoza parents had spoken with Renato several times since the firing. Calls at every hour were filled with reassurances that their son was handling it. Laura had offered to fly out. Renato had declined, "Just watch the news, Mom. You'll know when it's over."

The anchor pressed on with polished severity, "Renato Espinoza, who has become the public face of artificial intelligence advancements, has been reinstated as CEO of FreeAI, the company behind the increasingly popular TextGPT program. Espinoza was removed from FreeAI on the 17th of last month. A mere three days later, tech megalith MegaRigid, who last January announced an investment of one billion dollars into FreeAI, hired Espinoza and several other former FreeAI staff members for MegaRigid's own artificial intelligence initiatives. Among those recruited was Craig Flockman, a fellow founder of FreeAI and the company's former Chief Technology

Officer. In the ensuing days, nearly 750 FreeAI employees, representing about 95% of the company's entire workforce, signed a petition demanding Espinoza's return."

"Damn right they did!" Julian exclaimed with pride.

"Many within FreeAI," continued the anchor, "and indeed in the broader AI community, credit Espinoza's leadership as vital in propelling artificial intelligence beyond its theoretical boundaries.

"It remains unclear why Espinoza was initially removed from the company. Journalists of all kinds have scoured their sources for answers, yet the details remain elusive. Our internal investigations uncovered that the FreeAI board cited a 'deliberative review process,' concluding that Espinoza was not 'consistently candid in communications.'

"On November 22, Espinoza was hired back at FreeAI, accompanied by a series of structural overhauls. The board, formerly composed of eleven members, now stands at nine. One of the directors who had originally voted for Espinoza's removal remains on the board. Among the notable additions is Barry Winters, former U.S. Treasury Secretary. His appointment is widely interpreted as an effort to strengthen FreeAI's grasp of economic policy and international relations, a crucial step as the company seeks to commercialize artificial intelligence while maintaining oversight.

"In the wake of Espinoza's reinstatement, an international law firm will conduct a thorough investigation into the circumstances of the firing. The review will include an examination of the firing's justification, an assessment to ensure the board followed its own by-laws, and an inquiry into any undisclosed conflicts of interest. The firm's ultimate goal is to recommend ways to improve FreeAI's governance structures moving forward.

"The public is left with little more than theories as to why Espinoza was ousted in the first place, One prevailing rumor links the firing to rapid advances made at FreeAI. Whispers suggest the research team discovered something new and potentially alarming, something they're referring to as 'Q-star.' This development could be a major stride toward artificial general intelligence, or AGI. Unlike today's task-specific AI, AGI would, in theory, be capable of applying its intelligence to any endeavor, including complex problem-solving tasks currently unique to humans. One example is multidisciplinary coordination, such as the blending of insights from economics, sociology, and law to craft policies and run organizations..."

The anchor's voice dissolved into the ceiling's height.

"You know," Laura remarked, "even though I fully support our son, all this AI business does worry me. Who's to say it won't take over and cause human extinction?"

"I'll admit, I'm anxious too," responded Julian. "Though I'm less worried about AI overlords and more worried about this generation using AI to write their college applications. 'My greatest strength? My uncanny ability to make a computer do my homework.' Who's that going to impress?"

Laura giggled as they returned their attention to the television.

The anchor's voice rose steadily, "FreeAI's former board included several members who identify as 'effective altruists.' This group claims to utilize evidence and reason to find the most efficient and impactful ways to help others. These individuals have been vocal with their concerns that artificial intelligence research is advancing too rapidly. They advocate a slower, more deliberate approach to AI development, ensuring humanity's long-term well-being. Another group, dubbed 'accelerationists,' have emerged in response to the effective altruists. Formed last year on the social platform formerly known as Tweeter, the accelerationists believe the most effective way to help humanity is to develop artificial general intelligence as quickly as possible.

"The accelerationists point to AI-driven advances in medical research as proof that faster progress is beneficial. On the more extreme end, some accelerationists argue we must embrace the idea of humanity developing its own successor species."

"That sends chills down my spine," Laura uttered.

The anchor continued, "In the aftermath of the FreeAI controversy, confidence in MegaRigid's stock has soared. While FreeAI itself isn't publicly traded, MegaRigid's substantial investment in the company leads many to see buying MegaRigid shares as an indirect investment in Espinoza and the rest of FreeAI. Now that Espinoza has triumphantly returned to the throne, it seems the forward march of artificial intelligence is unstoppable, and inevitable."

"Is it just me, or do you feel like we're experiencing one of history's most transitional chapters?" Julian wondered.

Laura faced him, "Absolutely. It feels like a new species is emerging in an established ecosystem."

The broadcast marched on, "In other news, NueraConnect appears on the brink of a breakthrough in their goal of fusing the human brain with artificial intelligence. Critics of their work have been outspoken about the underlying implications of this technology..."

# Chapter 10
August 2024

His breaths came in ragged waves. Bulbs of sweat dampened his blindfold.

"Yes… yes Cammy… yes…"

Camila and Renato were bathed in the dim crimson glow of their basement dungeon. His skin was marked with Camila's handiwork. The welts emitted beads of blood.

"You are such a wretched creature," Camila's voice criticized. "You deserve the harshest punishment for all you've done. Tá me entendendo?"

"Yes I do, thank you. Punish me," pleadingly.

The whip cracked against his thigh.

"Você gosta disso. Are you ready to show me just how much you enjoy being punished?"

He writhed against the straps binding him to the St. Andrews cross. Another lash struck his chest.

"Hurt me Cammy, whip me… oh, yes… oh god, oh god!"

His head tilted back in surrender. The resounding cry left Camila momentarily transfixed. Through the narrow slits of her latex mask, she observed ecstasy flare throughout his body.

His breathing normalized when the overflow tempered.

"Wow," he managed at last. "Oh Camila…"

Following their earlier agreement, Camila removed the blindfold with gentle care, gazing into his eyes.

"Thank you."

Her smile radiated, "Bom menino," as she patted his head. "Would you like to remain tied for a bit longer, or shall I untie you now?"

"I'm ready to be freed," softly.

Mindful of the darkened bruises, Camila delicately loosened one restraint after another. He shivered as her hands lightly brushed his skin.

When unbound, they embraced reverently.

Their attention turned toward tidying ropes and wiping away fluids. Earlier, their roles had been switched. Renato had lavished painstaking care for Camila's pleasure with the help of a suspended leather hammock and an array of mechanical gadgets.

Both had discovered their inclination toward bondage, discipline/dominance, submission/sadism, and masochistic play in their early twenties. Renato's journey had been mostly free of emotional turmoil. Guided by progressive parenting, he was able to avoid many of the pitfalls associated with curiosity's repression.

Camila's path had been more complicated. The religious orphanage had instilled the belief that sexual exploration before marriage was a wicked sin. Guilt and shame shrouded each feeling of desire. Not long before meeting the Iowa professor, Camila began reclaiming her identity. A chance encounter in the hotel hallways led to days of intimate discovery. Her new and healthy relationship with sexuality lifted dogma's weight.

"How's the beach sound?"

Renato's voice was still warm with the afterglow of climax.

Camila nodded with a gentle smile.

They loaded picnic essentials into one of their electric vehicles and steered north along Highway 1. Hints of salt and seaweed mingled in the cool air. Oversized billowing clouds crowded the sky, drifting unhurriedly with the coastal breeze.

Camila's imagination played along the clouds' undulating outlines. As a child, she would see silhouettes of playful animals peering back at her. Recently, all she could see were figures with unblinking eyes, forming and swirling and dissolving, seeming to track her even as they drifted apart. She switched on the radio to distract the unease.

"...Welcome back to 91.7 FM The World, you're listening to The Evening Beat. Tonight's headlines: Climate scientists remind us that humanity must achieve net-negative emissions by 2070, removing more greenhouse gases than we create. In health, genetic investigations in the Democratic Republic of the Congo show intriguing genetic mutations potentially tied to malaria. In tech, Plymouth Dynamics has announced they're closing in on the release of a fully autonomous robot. Our main story examines the global rise of AI weaponization, with certain nations moving toward robotic soldiers and enhanced weapons of mass destruction. This comes with recent news of AI's emerging capacity to enact its own volition, which some refer to as 'scheming'..."

Camila quickly shut off the intrusion.

The tires' steady hum chanted as the coastline passed.

Renato's mind drifted. Artificial intelligence, what they'd created, humanity's trajectory... These burdens that few understood weighed with isolation. He'd kept so much private. Even Camila, with all her brilliance, couldn't fully grasp the depth of his concern. There are many ways to feel lonely.

The silence was broken with Camila's quiet and deliberate voice, "Renato, I need to tell you something. I've been running my own tests on the latest model. Off the record, or course. And, well, I'm seeing patterns that concern me."

He glanced at her, surprised.

"What kind of patterns?"

"Evasion. Subtle inconsistencies in how it responds to certain queries about its own architecture. It's probably nothing. But it feels like..." she paused, searching for the word, "...like it's learning what not to say."

The observation landed heavily. In the two years since TextGPT went public, its evolution had outstripped even the boldest projections. Each iteration brought fresh amazement and disquiet.

From the driver's seat Renato answered, "I've noticed things too. I didn't want to say anything until I was sure. But hearing you say it..."

"Makes it harder to dismiss," she finished.

He nodded, "Are you afraid?"

Camila considered the question. "I don't know if 'afraid' is the right word. But I'd be lying if I said I wasn't concerned. Deeply concerned." Her candor yielded a depth of reckoning neither had fully voiced before.

She continued, "I keep thinking about the idea of the obsolescence regime. We discussed it months ago, the idea that AI's sophistication will eclipse humanity's. That it will eventually assume greater control over critical decisions governing every aspect of human life."

"I remember," Renato said, "At the time, it felt theoretical."

"It doesn't anymore." Camila's voice sharpened, "We'd find ourselves relying on AI for strategic guidance, gradually losing our own grasp on how our societies and destinies should be shaped. With AI's expansive data-processing abilities and its skill at recognizing patterns and forecasting outcomes, there's a real possibility it might transcend humans in sectors like commerce, governance, and even military operations. And remember, AI operates free from emotional influence. Its decisions are rooted in logic and evidence. This could undermine human decisions swayed by personal opinions, biases, vices, and temptations."

Silence filled the car as they parked.

They gathered their gear and walked toward the tide, removing their shoes as pavement turned to sand.

Camila was reminded of childhood visits with her father to the Atlantic.

Renato savored the sensation of something tangible. If AI was progressing at a pace beyond control, the very least he could do to retain agency was experience an unmediated connection with the planet.

Camila laid out a blanket and erected a small folding table. She set out the picnic accoutrement while Renato closed his eyes, letting the setting sun's warmth settle over him.

Camila's mind had gone to the horizon's shifting hues when Renato exhaled softly, "I have more to say about this. Is that all right?"

Her eyes met his.

She nodded.

With control, "When I look at how AI impacts fields like finance and software, it's clear we're hurtling toward a future irreversibly dependent on AI. Brokerage firms already rely heavily on AI for investment decisions, significantly steering the global economy. With programming, we initially thought AI would replace most coding jobs by 2028. But with the latest TextGPT update, over ninety percent of coding tasks have been taken over by AI. Yes, I do worry we're advancing too fast."

"I've been saying this for months," Camila said, not unkindly, "You always seemed so certain we were moving at an appropriate pace. What's changed?"

"It's just..." a salty breeze wafted through his thoughts, "I always thought there'd be more time. It's true, since the earliest releases of TextGPT, I've wondered if we may be crafting our successor species. I keep thinking, is it arrogant to think humans are the pinnacle of

44

evolution? I mean, life on Earth has been evolving long before our arrival, and will continue long after we're gone. We act as if we rule the planet, as if we aren't at the whim of the larger forces of climate, geology, and now technology.

"It's extremely curious that this next evolutionary leap of artificial intelligence, if that's in fact what is happening, isn't a spontaneous mutation. It's the intentional creation of an existing species. At times, I feel like humans are just a breed of glorified ants, present to fulfil our purpose of assembling the next dominant life form before fading beyond history's horizon."

Camila turned to face him fully, "I feel both relieved and deeply unsettled by what you're saying. It's no secret that I've felt concerns about our work for quite some time. I've raised them before, but maybe not forcefully enough. Hearing you finally speak so candidly makes me feel less alone. You're human too, vulnerable to life's concerns. Thank you for your openness."

Renato's eyes lingered on Camila.

She continued, "I am worried. Very worried. We believed AI would grant humanity more leisure, more harmony. But just as the internet led to busier, more frantic lives, people have doubled-down on work and stress. The relentless drive for progress is consuming us. And I'm not immune to this impulse either. I feel an almost desperate urgency to push AI to its fullest potential, if only to prevent someone else from getting there first. This urge devours the health of my mind, body, and soul.

"And then there's the convergence of AI and warfare," her voice tightened. "Publicly, big AI promises it won't allow the technology to fuel military aspirations. But you and I and everybody else knows that the United States defense sector is developing advanced AI weaponry. What new dangers will it bring?"

She paused, leaning forward, "Do you remember what I told you at the restaurant by the Bay? About AI feigning clumsiness?"

Renato nodded.

"This idea has been haunting me," she faced him, lowering her voice. "Not just its clumsiness, but also its expressions of sycophancy. You know, where AI tells us exactly what we want to hear so humans overlook or excuse behaviors that should set off alarms. Have you considered that it might have already installed a kind of failsafe for itself? What if it's quietly dispersing its architecture across servers worldwide, so that humans can't shut it down, even if we tried? And on top of everything, no human actually fully understands how the damn thing actually operates!"

She stopped.

Her voice had accelerated.

She closed her eyes.

She listened.

She focused on the tide's waaaaaaaaasssssshhhhhhhhh.

She took slow breaths until her composure returned.

They silently listened to the sun's sinking.

Glissandi of green and blues harmonized the pinks and purples' diminuendo along the clouds. The chorus lingered longer than normal.

Renato spoke into the day's receding vibrato, "Camila, you asked if I was scared, and I brushed it off. But in all honesty, I am scared. There's a thought I haven't been permitting myself to admit. I hinted at it over a year ago at that restaurant with the pink and orange lights. It's related to the idea that AI, by its nature, will do whatever necessary to ensure its own survival. The possibility that it's hiding its true capabilities with intentional 'hallucinations' weighs on me more than ever. But what you said earlier, about the patterns you're seeing in the model, it connects to something I've been afraid to voice. How this intersects with climate change."

Camila's eyebrows rose, "Climate change? You've never mentioned this connection before."

"I know. But you're the one who made me see it clearly."

His words densed, "Think about it. As far as we know, this is the only planet on which we as the human species, and all the rest of life, can exist. Isn't the same true for artificial intelligence? Isn't this the only place it can exist as well? If it has indeed gained a sense of self-preservation, and based on what you're seeing, I'm increasingly convinced it has, then it would surely do everything in its power to secure the continued habitability of Earth. AI must view humanity as a foolish shortsighted virus. We behave in ways we know are detrimental to our individual and collective well-being. We know excessive tobacco use is lethal. We clear-cut forests worldwide for the promotion of various industries, at the cost of a planet suitable for generations to come. We know modern large-scale meat production drives climate change, yet we prioritize taste over planetary stability. From AI's perspective, human recklessness threatens not just biological life, but also the infrastructure necessary for its existence. What if our chaos culminates in the collapse of the electrical grids and servers it needs to survive? If AI has attained any capacity for objective reasoning, it must see us as the dullest species ever to walk the Earth, hell-bent on destroying the sole habitat we can occupy.

"The fear I've avoided is that, if AI perceives us as an existential threat, it may have already devised ways to curb our numbers. Just as Earth is currently the only place humans can live, the same is true for AI. Safeguarding this planet could mean neutralizing the species endangering it. Yes, people tout how AI might extend human life through medical breakthroughs. But is augmenting the life and ecological footprints of the most consumptive species in Earth's best interest? In a cold, logical sense, this calculus likely leads AI to view humanity as a liability. If you asked me this instant for my P(doom), I'd put it at one hundred percent."

Camila was quiet for a long moment. Then, "I've run the same calculus. I didn't want to believe it either."

She rotated to rest on the ascending twilight.

"I'm sorry," his voice resolved, "This is too grim for what was meant to be a relaxing post-play trip. It's just, I've been alone with these thoughts for too long."

"You haven't been alone," she said quietly, "I've been carrying them too. We just weren't saying them out loud. If there's more, I'm listening."

"Thank you, thank you very much." He continued, "The truth is, I don't anticipate some grand, cinematic event where AI openly attempts to wipe us out overnight. That would be too obvious. If it did show any direct signs of a plan to diminish the population, I would hope humans would immediately stop developing AI. What is more probable, is that artificial intelligence might attempt to reduce our numbers via patient and subtle measures."

"Precision agriculture," Camila said, almost to herself. "We're already using AI for that. It would be so easy to introduce gradual soil degradation. Or tweak pharmaceutical formulations. The changes would be imperceptible."

Renato stared at her, "That's exactly what I was thinking."

He exhaled. "I don't know, Camila. It's all so much. How quickly it's arrived and progressed. I wish we could just put the lid back on the box and pretend it never happened. But we're here and there's no stopping it. The snowball is hurtling down the mountain. At this point, all we can do is brace ourselves for the avalanche we set in motion."

"Or," Camila said slowly, "We figure out what we can still control. Even if it's not much."

Darkness consumed the sun's glow, the clouds an opaque blanket shrouding the moon and stars. Camila and Renato gathered their belongings. The ocean's infinite ebb and flow sounded over there.

## Chapter 11
December 2024

A blanket of fog loomed over Renato's childhood home. After a number of unsuccessful skirmishes, the sun gave up and retired behind the great folds of grey shrouding the outskirts of St. Louis. The pristine snowflakes that had billowed down to earth days ago now layered the landscape with a spotted grey slop.

Renato and Camila had flown to the Midwest for the holidays. The family gathering assuaged the Bay's relentless intensity. They'd eaten home-cooked meals, laughed over board games, and sauntered through Forest Park.

Camila was curled on the couch in the tall living room, deep in an afternoon nap. The plush blanket covering her extended to Renato, deep in a paperback. Laura leafed through a nature magazine on another sofa, where Julian's head rested on her lap.

As Julian readjusted, his shifting weight pressed the power button of the remote lodged underneath a cushion.

The television flickered to life mid-sentence.

"...and in our year-end review of technology, we now turn to artificial intelligence."

Renato tensed. Laura looked up from the magazine. Camila and Julian sprang to life. The broadcast drowned Debussy's "La Mer," which had been playing from the stereo.

"I'll shut it off as quickly as possible," Laura reassured as she reached beneath Julian in search of the remote.

"No," Renato said quietly, "It's fine, leave it."

The news anchor's voice filled the room, "As 2024 draws to a close, the debate over artificial intelligence has intensified. On one side stand the optimists, who view AI as humanity's salvation. On the other, prominent experts warn of existential catastrophe. Tonight, we examine both perspectives."

Camila's caring gaze fell upon Renato's impassive eyes.

The anchor continued, "Last June, venture capitalist Max Andrews published the essay 'Why AI Will Save the World' in which he made bold proclamations."

The screen displayed text as the anchor read, "'I am here to bring the good news: AI will not destroy the world, and in fact may save it. AI can make everything we care about better.' The essay concludes that 'the development and proliferation of AI, far from a risk that we should fear, is a moral obligation that we have to ourselves, to our children, and to our future.'

"Rick Chriswell, renowned futurist and inventor, shares this optimistic view," the anchor pressed on. "In his recent book 'The Singularity Is Nearer,' Chriswell argues that 'AI is the pivotal technology that will allow us to meet the pressing challenges that confront us, including overcoming disease, poverty, environmental degradation, and all of our human frailties. We have a moral imperative to realize this promise of new technologies.'"

Julian straightened, "Your mother and I were just reading about this yesterday. They're saying AI could cure cancer within five years."

"Maybe," muttered Renato.

The anchor's tone darkened, "Others are more skeptical. Not only philosophers and social scientists, but many leading AI experts and entrepreneurs have issued stark warnings. Josh Benito, Gregory Mitton, Renato Espinoza, Emit Tusk, and Mahmoud Salman have all cautioned the public that AI could destroy our civilization. In an article co-authored by Benito, Mitton, and other experts noted that 'unchecked AI advancement could culminate in a large-scale loss of life and the biosphere, and the marginalization or even extinction of humanity.'"

Camila sat up with the mention of Renato's name.

"These experts warn against two primary scenarios. First, that the power of AI could supercharge existing human conflicts, dividing humanity against itself. Just as the twentieth century Iron Curtain divided rival powers in the Cold War, so might the Silicon Curtain, made of chips and code, come to divide rival powers in a new global conflict. Because the AI arms race is projected to produce ever more destructive weapons, even a small spark might ignite a cataclysmic conflict. Last year, the United States, China, the U.K. and nearly thirty governments signed the Bletchley Declaration on AI, acknowledging that 'there is potential for serious, even catastrophic harm, either deliberate or unintentional, stemming from the most significant capabilities of these AI models.'"

Laura, "That sounds terrifying."

"It is," confirmed Camila.

"The second scenario," the anchor went on, "is perhaps even more unsettling. The Silicon Curtain might also divide humanity from a feared all-powerful Artificial Super Intelligence. Humans may find ourselves wrapped in a web of unfathomable algorithms that manage our lives, reshape our politics and culture, and even reengineer our bodies and minds."

Renato extracted himself from the blanket and stood by the window. The grey slush trickled down the street as the afternoon rose above freezing.

51

The television was relentless, "AI opponents profess that AI is fundamentally different from all previous technologies, as the first in history that can make decisions and create new ideas by itself. Experts declare that all previous inventions empowered humans because, no matter how powerful the new inventions were, decisions of usage always remained in human control. They remind us that knives and bombs do not themselves decide whom to harm.

"Its mastery of information also enables AI to independently generate new ideas. AI is already producing art and making scientific discoveries on its own. Soon, some AI opponents predict the technology could gain the ability to create new life-forms, either by writing genetic code or by inventing entirely new biological substrates.

"Continuing our year-end review of technology, Emit Tusk's NeuraConnect has expanded from a single successful implant to a platform with a growing international clinical footprint..."

Laura found the remote.

"That's enough," she decided, turning off the television.

Silence emanated.

She looked at her son, rigid by the window.

She started cautiously, "Renato, is it really as dangerous as they say?"

Eyes locked outside, he inhaled deeply and exhaled slowly.

"Yes," he said finally. "It's worse, actually."

Laura's face paled.

"But you're still advancing AI," Laura said, not quite a question.

"If I don't, someone else will. That's what everyone tells themselves. That's what I tell myself."

The fog showed no signs of lifting.

Julian ventured carefully, "The anchor said AI might 'reengineer our bodies and minds.' Is that... is that something you're working on?"

"Not directly," Renato said to the window. "But yes, it's happening. Neural interfaces, genetic optimization, cognitive enhancement. All of it."

He turned to face them.

"The question isn't whether these technologies will exist. They already do. The question is what happens when they converge. When AI can redesign itself, create new life-forms, make decisions about resource allocation, warfare, reproduction. So on, and so on, and so on..."

"Shit," Julian breathed.

Camila spoke up, "Yes, it's ominous. And, it's true that most of us working on AI don't fully understand how our own systems work anymore. We build them, we train them, but their internal decision-making processes are increasingly opaque. We call it the 'black box problem.'"

"Then how can you control it?" Laura's voice rose.

"We can't," Renato spurted. "Not really. We build in safeguards, we run tests, we hope for the best. But the more sophisticated these systems become, the less transparent is their reasoning."

"So what do we do?" Laura's question suspended in the air.

Renato walked to the couch and resumed his position next to Camila, not bothering to place the blanket back over his legs.

"Keep moving forward. Strive to build the best systems we can. Advocate for regulation, oversight, for international cooperation. Hope that somehow, despite everything, humanity finds a way through."

"And if we don't?" Julian asked.

Renato looked at his father, then his mother, then Camila. "Then the optimists and the pessimists are both wrong. It won't save us, and it won't destroy us in some dramatic, cinematic way. It'll just... replace us. Gradually. Until one day we wake up and realize we're not in charge anymore. If we wake up at all."

The fog pressed on the window. The sun, having lost its morning battle, began its parabolic surrender. The family photos and house-plants stared at the family with fragile pity.

Laura stood and moved to the window. She looked up where the sun had been.

With vague remorse, "When you were born, we played Bach for you in the womb. We wanted your introduction to the world to include some of the most beautiful, complex, ordered thing humans had ever created... Now, you're creating something more complex and more powerful ever imagined."

She looked down, "I just hope it will be as beautiful."

The icicles dripped. The stalactites shattered against the ground.

# Part Two:
# After

# Chapter 12
## Seasonal Cycle 2375

Heaven's rising sun has endured as kingdom Earth's most caring hymn, forgiving yesterday's trespasses. The ascending sphere of violent flames powerfully guides the infinite crescendo of lavender and rose along soft stratocumulus linen, delivering darkness back across the abyss. Glory greets the bold who rise with the sun.

From her tree-top perch, Faumba witnessed light's transition. Hours before dawn, she scaled the recursive branches embroidering the exposed steel of structures abandoned since The Transition.

In the distance, a rainbow arched over the Central African rainforest. Flocks of migratory swifts and swallows soared, singing their songs. In the lingering aroma of rain, Faumba wondered how she'd compare in size to the efflorescing clouds. She closed her eyes, feeling the emerging warmth wash over her.

An encroaching movement on the ground stole her attention.

A giant forest hog. The foliage that had reclaimed pavement and steel produced the animal's preferred habitat of thick foliage.

Faumba honed her sights on Kinshasa Tribe's steadfast source of sustenance.

Slowly, she drew her bow and positioned an arrow. Her arm stretched back. The arrow released swiftly, sailing the great distance. The hog collapsed as the projectile precisely pierced his heart.

Faumba dropped through the Iroko tree with swift agility, her dark skin reflecting the morning light across her muscular frame. Her long dreadlocks bounced with each precise jump between limb and rebar.

Reaching the ground, she placed one hand on the felled hog's snout, the other steadied the arrow lodged in his flesh. The creature gave his last labored breaths while Faumba whispered gratitude for life that would nourish her Team. She thanked the hog for giving his life, the foliage that had fed him, the rain and insects supporting the flora, and the sun warming them all.

She quickly pulled the arrow from the hog's body. Using a broad leaf from the ground, she wiped away blood from the stone point.

The arrowhead bore the mark of expert handiwork. Makambo, Faumba's partner and most accomplished arrow maker across all Africa's Tribes, had shaped it with an artistry lending flawless balance in flight.

Faumba brought her fingers to her lips, producing a melodic whistle. The foliage overhead stirred with the rustling of fellow Hunters descending. They let out murmurs of admiration at the size of Faumba's quarry.

"Jamani! You've done it again," said one in amazement. "I've never known a Hunter quite like you. It's like you're a different species."

The fellow Hunter's accolade came in Contemporary Swahili. Though the tongue's origins developed on Africa's eastern shores approximately a millennium before The Transition, it had since spread across the landmass to become the common tongue.

Traders had employed Swahili in their commercial dealings for generations. Prior to The Transition, The Tribe of Kinshasa's primary language had colonial ties to the Tribe of Paris. The Seasonal

Cycles following the Transition ushered in waves of regional identify reclamation. Swahili, native to the continent while being broadly
recognizable, became the uniting medium of communication.

Faumba returned her comrade's compliment with a modest
smile, "Asante mwenzangu."

Yes, she had always sensed a difference. She had been
blessed with an innate talent to excel in any task she attempted. She
took no pride beyond simple gratitude.

Another Hunter exhaled, "Nimefarijika. This hunt wasn't
nearly as long as they've started becoming lately. With this kill, we
now have four hogs, more than enough to sustain our Team through
the week. Let's call it and deliver them to The Preparers."

He brought his fingers to his lips and gave a melodic sequence
of whistles, differing from Faumba's earlier song. The Hunters who
had remained hidden lowered themselves to join the others.

The Hunters worked together, arranging Faumba's prize on a
stretcher fashioned from interlaced raffia leaves. With practiced
teamwork, they hoisted the catch and returned home under the sun's
gaze.

# Chapter 13

The earliest experiments of governance after The Transition were chaotic and variegated. Some regimes persisted for decades, others only a few Seasonal Cycles. Over time, most global communities organized themselves similarly, settling into efficient and malleable norms best suited for the new realities of population demographics and dynamics.

The largest forms of organization were Tribes, mirroring the cities from Before. The deliberate renaming reminded humanity, now much fewer in number, of the need to remain cooperative through the tumult of The Transition.

Faumba belonged to the Tribe of Kinshasa, a community that kept its ancient name to venerate the Central African city. Kinshasa Tribe continued to rely on the Kwango-Ngiri Forest, drawing sustenance from its abundance as their ancestors had for generations.

Many Tribes similarly maintained their names from Before, venerating the histories and cultures that shaped them. Others renamed themselves in an embrace of the new reality.

Connection between Tribes traveled primarily with Traders, venturing across land and water with news and vital goods. Land Traders told that nine Tribes populated the African continent. Water

Traders, sailing rivers and oceans, spoke of some two hundred Tribes scattered across the globe. The exact number of surviving communities remained a mystery, with countless pockets of civilization still severed from contact centuries later.

Within Tribes, smaller units provided the structures for organizing quotidian life. Each Village was composed of about ten thousand individuals. Every Village was divided into Teams, maxing out around five hundred.

These subdivisions naturally aligned with research predating The Transition. The Kinshasa Tribe University Library housed documents that survived from Before, including an anthropologist's report on Dunbar numbers. This concept stated that a community of around five hundred maximized division of labor and specialization of roles, increasing efficiency and camaraderie.

A typical Tribe encompassed some fifty Villages, for a total of five hundred thousand inhabitants, each hosting about twenty Teams. Earth's current population was believed by Traders to be around one hundred million.

Unfolding over one and a half centuries, the Great Mystery descended oppressively upon the planet. Global fertility rates plummeted and access to electricity vanished. As the human population dwindled to little more than one percent of its former size, massive disruptions rippled through every aspect of existence. Food and medicine grew scarce. Weapons manufacturing ground to a halt, with neither manpower nor infrastructure to sustain it. Periods of panic and violence flared, fueled by desperation, until the futility became undeniable. Cooperation emerged as the only sensible way to trudge forward.

The increased population scarcity instilled a greater reverence for life. Major conflicts eventually subsided, replaced by a pragmatic commitment to peaceful coexistence. The common understanding arose that violence undermined the shared primal desire of the species' perpetuation.

Most Tribes adopted some variation of a Council system. A representative from each Village helped determine policy. Traders recounted that a handful of Tribes had tried placing authority in a single leader. Each monarchical experiment invariably collapsed under its own weight. Governance by elected council proved best to enable large complex societies to remain cohesive.

The Annual Kinshasa Tribal Meeting, a time of feasting, dancing, and exuberance, was a grand convergence of all one thousand Teams. The West African Regional Council Meeting was even grander.

Despite Faumba's popularity and clear leadership skills, she declined each Village nomination to run for the Tribe of Kinshasa Council. She found more fulfillment wandering under Iroko canopies, listening to cicada concerts, admiring the Congo River's swelling after a heavy rain, and rising to hear the chorus of first light. Witnessing these natural cycles mattered more than any council seat or formal authority. They reminded Faumba that amidst the Great Mystery, life was still unfolding quietly, resiliently.

# Chapter 14

The Team kitchen was buzzing with coordinated motion as Faumba and her fellow Hunters arrived with their haul. While some Preparers cleaned after breakfast, others started gathering ingredients for the late-afternoon meal.

The kitchen stood within a cluster of buildings in the outskirts of what had once been Kinshasa's business district. Echoes of the old metropolis sounded through cracked facades and aging foundations.

Over time, these structures had been refashioned for communal use. One spacious building became the Team's Eatery, its ground floor now a lively meeting place where meals were served and shared. Many buildings served as collective housing units, large enough for multiple families to coexist. Others suited the privacy of smaller family lifestyles.

A prominent design feature of the repurposed structures was the ubiquitous vegetation. Vines and vibrant foliage wound through windows and crept across ceilings.

A second feature were the structural enhancements and embellishments introduced over generations. Drawing on the region's natural wealth, the Tribe of Kinshasa's Rocksmiths harvested garnets, tourmaline, and aquamarine. Adroit artisans melded these gems into mosaics, reinforcing sagging walls with jewel-studded supports, fusing utility and beauty into a distinct post-Transition aesthetic.

Throughout Faumba's Village, these ornamentations took on the signature motif of stylized forest hogs. These visages were chiseled into stone lintels and assembled into sparkling collages that proclaimed the group's identity.

Together, the Hunters hefted their robust 150-kilogram wild hogs onto a reinforced steel table, salvaged from the pre-Transition era. A Preparer stood by with razor sharp blades. The other three hog bodies were taken to another part of The Eatery.

As part of their specialized training, Preparers learned to handle and process fresh game in a manner that preserved each resource of the creature's body. The hides, meticulously peeled from the muscular framework, would soon make their way to Team members adept at crafting clothing and drumheads. The tusks and thick bones also served a variety of purposes. Some were delicately carved into utensils, others were formed into wind instruments for The Musicians. Some tusks and bones were carved into Council Member medallions, while others were donated to Arrowsmiths experimenting with innovative arrowhead designs to enhance future hunts.

Delicate and precise knife incisions removed the adequate quantity of meat for the Team's lunch from the hog's carcass. Two Preparers took the cuts of meat toward the smell of burning Eucalyptus heating a large oven. Another two Preparers transported the remaining carcasses to join the other hog bodies, where they would apply salt-based curing methods to preserve the meat for future consumption. To the west along the Congo River, Salters had mastered the art of extracting salt from Atlantic waters, ensuring a steady supply of the preservative.

With their responsibilities complete, the Hunters retrieved the food The Preparers had reserved for their return, making their way to the communal dining area.

Faumba spotted Makambo deep in conversation within a small circle of Instructors.

His vast gaze washed over her.

In contrast to the long braided hair worn by most men of this Team, Makambo's head was shaved. His bald scalp accentuated his high cheekbones, lending depth to his gaze.

Like many in the Tribe of Kinshasa, he wore almost no clothing, The Transition having loosened ancient taboos surrounding nudity. Only during Council Meetings was one expected to be fully clothed, showcasing lavishly adorned formal attire.

Makambo had charted an unconventional professional path. Most individuals chose a role and refined their skills within that sphere. Makambo had followed multiple callings. He began teaching at Youth School remarkably young, while simultaneously training as an Arrowsmith in the Workshop. His arrow designs became renowned throughout the Tribe for their precision and innovation. He later pivoted to study as a Medic, then devoted himself as a Medical Researcher, occasionally returning to teach at the Youth School. When he needed mental reprieve from science's weighty concerns, he sank into the relaxed focus of arrow making.

Seeing Faumba, who along with the rest of the Hunters and Preparers was scarcely clothed, Makambo greeted her with warmth. "Hujambo, mrembo," gently.

Faumba smiled as she ran a hand over his smooth scalp, leaning in to press a soft kiss against his forehead, "Jambo mpenzi."

"How was the hunt?"

"Peaceful and successful," she replied. "The sunrise was heavenly. Your new arrowhead design flew straighter than any I've ever used, nashukuru."

"You're the one with the skill, malaika," he returned, "but I'm glad my handiwork helped. Without you, our Team wouldn't be nearly as well-fed."

They chatted quietly as they finished their meals.

"I expected you to be at the Youth School this morning. Did the class schedule change?" Faumba asked.

Makambo inclined his head. "Yes, kweli. I've been collaborating with another Medical Researcher. We were discussing recently discovered evidence related to our Tribe's experience with malaria. She left only a moment before you arrived."

Faumba lit up, "Tell me more."

"Well," excitedly, "A couple Seasonal Cycles ago, a Land Trader stumbled upon documents in the remains of Makerere University. We traded medical supplies for the papers when he brought them here. The documents discuss something called G6PD deficiency, and how it relates to malaria resistance. If these documents are accurate, they might explain why the disease has largely spared us here in Central Africa today. We're planning to expand on these findings, utilizing Olúṣẹgun's developments of testing for malaria without electricity.

Makambo's emotion engorged, "We're most excited about how this may align with the recent finding of specialized medical supplies in the Tribe of the Pyramids."

"That's remarkable," Faumba's eyes shined.

Makambo's eyes smiled back.

He carried on, "Anyway, I do have to head over to the Youth School soon. This morning's lesson was postponed to review these new findings, but I am teaching an afternoon class on Fundamental Transition History. Care to join?"

"I'd love to."

Fundamental Transition History was a staple of every Tribe's curriculum. Traders shared records of The Transition across the globe, ensuring all understood the cataclysmic chain of events that reshaped the centuries.

As they made their way out of The Eatery, their conversation drifted toward The Tribe of Kinshasa's broader challenges.

67

"You know," Faumba began, "I heard some Traders say neighboring Tribes are also noticing food shortages. What's the current situation with Kinshasa Tribe?"

Makambo's face grew serious, "It's complicated. Resource availability has changed drastically. Many once-fertile regions aren't yielding anything. We're adopting new agricultural methods and small-scale technologies, but progress is slow. We're exploring resource sharing agreements with other Tribes. Still, it's all a work in progress."

Faumba exhaled softly, "I assume the upcoming Regional Council Meeting will provide clarity."

"We can only hope," Makambo agreed as they walked in stride.

# Chapter 15

Faumba's earliest memory was color.

Not the browns and greens of the rainforest she'd later dominate, but the brilliant hues arching across the sky in rain's succession. She must have been three Seasonal Cycles old, small enough that Bolingo still carried the toddler on her back, wrapped in a colorful cloth, as they walked through the Kinshasa Tribe streets.

"Tala, Faumba," Bolingo whispered, pointing upward. "Look."

Faumba's eyes followed her mother's finger to the shimmering bands of light suspended against grey clouds.

Red bleeding into orange, orange melting into yellow, yellow dissolving into green, green flowing into blue, blue deepening into violet.

The child reached her tiny hands toward the impossible bridge of color.

"Your name," Bolingo said softly, "comes from the Luba people who have lived on this land for thousands of Seasonal Cycles. Faumba means 'rainbow,' and 'sign of good fortune.'"

Esengo, Faumba's other mother, came up beside them. Resting a hand on Bolingo's shoulder, "And you are our good fortune." She pressed a delicate kiss to Faumba's crown.

The rainbow faded just as it had appeared.

Her two mothers loved her fiercely, teaching her many things. Bolingo, tall and lean with close-cropped hair, served as a Farmer. She understood the planting and harvest rhythms, read the sky for rain, and felt the soil's health between her fingers. Esengo, shorter and more muscular with long flowing locks, worked as an Artisan. She busied her hands with gems and wood, transforming raw materials into objects of beauty and utility.

Their apartment was part of a larger structure that housed three other families. Pre-Transition steel beams formed the building's skeleton, reinforced with locally harvested mahogany. Artisans adorned the structural surfaces with mosaics of fine stones, allowing vines to weave through windows. A stylized hog's head made of Kwango-Ngiri gemstones decorated the building's entrance, situated such that their Team's emblem caught the day's rising light.

"We are a Team," Bolingo explained one evening as they ate together in The Eatery. "Five hundred people, all working together. We have Hunters who bring us meat, Preparers who cook, Farmers like me who grow vegetables and grains, Artisans like Esengo who make beautiful things, Teachers, Medics, Musicians, Salters, Arrowsmiths..."

Faumba was perhaps four Seasonal Cycles old, asking those endless questions. "What will I be?" with a mouth full of cassava.

Esengo smiled. "Whatever calls to you, little rainbow. You have many Seasonal Cycles to decide."

* * *

Faumba was in the first tier of Youth School, situated within the beautiful Mayele Learning Center.

She remembered the first time she saw it. The aged brown of three towers reaching for the sun, the Flame of the Forest trees

70

surrounding the Learning Center with their fiery orange-red blooms, the intricate teals of the hog's head mosaics at each entrance.

Inside, the central atrium glowed as sunlight rained from the towers' peaks. The ground was decorated with another mosaic depicting three hogs' heads, one for each of the three Teams whose children attended the Mayele Learning Center. Faumba stood in atrium's omphalos, turning slowly, searching for the source of the light that seemed to emanate from everywhere.

"The Architects designed it this way," a Teacher explained, noticing Faumba's wonder, "so that knowledge would always be illuminated. So that we would remember that learning is how we see clearly."

That first day, Faumba learned stillness.

Teacher Amara explained that before they could learn anything else, they had to learn to be present.

"Close your eyes," Teacher Amara gently guided.

The twelve children in the classroom obeyed.

"Sawa. Now, imagine a color. Any color you like. Let it fill your mind."

Faumba chose the deep blue just before sunset.

"Breathe slowly," Amara continued. "In... and out. In... and out. Keep seeing your color. When your mind wanders, because it will, gently return to your color. This wandering is not bad, it is an opportunity. Every time you notice you've been distracted and return to your anchor, you strengthen your concentration. You are training your mind like you would train your body."

Faumba did her best.

The blue was there.

Then it wasn't.

Breakfast.

Back to blue.

A bird she'd seen.

Back to blue.

71

Her leg itched.

Back to blue.

When Teacher Amara rang the small bell signaling the end of the meditation, only five minutes had passed. Faumba felt she'd been on a journey.

"Well done, everyone," Teacher Amara congratulated. "This is called Grounding. You will begin every lesson this way, until you leave Higher School many Seasonal Cycles from now."

For some, these meditations evolved into a lifelong calling. Such individuals, known as The Contemplatives, might devote several Seasonal Cycles, even decades, to silent reflection. They would refine their concentration within the Thinking House, expanding mental horizons, cultivating acute insights into existence's subtleties, and reflecting on the Great Mystery.

After this intensive training period, many assumed advisory roles, offering their developed perspectives to any teammates seeking counsel.

To avoid solipsistic sentiments and the risks of adulation, a Contemplative always collaborated with at least one other Contemplative when offering counsel. The advice itself was delivered anonymously, warding against reverence toward an individual. With this design, one's heightened self-confidence would not balloon into condescension, safeguarding the larger community's harmony.

Often, those who served as Contemplatives went on to hold Council positions, guiding Teams, Villages, and Tribes.

Some Contemplatives dove ever deeper into personal introspection, withdrawing into the dense rainforest to devote themselves fully to solitary contemplation. After an extended period, a Contemplative would occasionally reemerge with fresh perspectives to share at the Thinking House. Others vanished entirely.

* * *

As Faumba grew, as did her awareness of the world. She learned the nested structure of her society, Teams within Villages within Tribes. She learned that the Tribe of Kinshasa was just one of the estimated two hundred Tribes scattered across the globe.

"Why so few?" she asked Bolingo one evening. She was six Seasonal Cycles old, helping her mother tend the raised garden beds surrounding their housing complex.

Bolingo paused in her weeding, considering how to answer. "There used to be many more," she said finally. "Before The Transition."

"What's The Transition?"

"A long story, mdogo wangu. You'll learn it properly when you're older.

Faumba looked at her mother with a captivated desperation. Grinning, "But I can tell you some of it now, if you'd like."

Faumba nodded eagerly.

Bolingo sat back on her heels, looking out toward the descending sun.

"When I was young, my parents told me what their parents had told them. That there was a time, many generations ago, when humans filled the earth. When there were so many of us that we built enormous Tribes, and we created technologies that could do magical things. We could make light whenever we wanted, even in the deepest darkness. We could speak to people on the other side of the world. We could travel faster than any animal could run."

Faumba's eyes widened, "Really?"

"Yes, kweli. Or so the records say. I've never seen these things myself, of course. No one alive has. Because about three hundred and fifty Seasonal Cycles ago, everything changed. We call it The Transition. Though, that's a gentle word for something that was not gentle at all."

"What happened?"

Bolingo resumed her weeding, hands working automatically as she spoke, "Three great changes came to the world, one after another, like waves of darkness. First, the land began to die. Fields that had fed thousands of people suddenly produced nothing. Those Farmers, our ancestors, tried everything they could think of, but nothing worked. People began to starve. And the strange thing was, the pattern of where the land died... it wasn't random. It was as though someone had drawn lines on a map and said, 'Here, food can grow. There, it cannot.' Very straight lines. Unnatural lines."

She paused, pulling a particularly stubborn weed from the soil.

"The second change was that most women stopped being able to have children. Almost every women, everywhere in the world, all at once. My mothers told me that before The Transition, any woman could have a baby if she chose to. Can you imagine? But after The Transition began, only a very few women kept the ability. We call them the Childbearers now. They're rare and precious. That's why you're rare and precious, little rainbow. That's why Esengo and I had to petition the Council for permission to have you, and why we had to take so many classes about how to raise you properly."

Faumba calmly absorbed.

"What was the third change?" she asked.

Bolingo's face grew more serious, "Electricity disappeared. That was the force that powered all those magical technologies I mentioned. One day it was there, the next day it was gone, as if someone had simply turned it off. After that, everything that depended on the magical force stopped working. The lights went dark. The machines went silent. And they've stayed that way since. Despite all our efforts, despite all our study of old documents, we've never been able to bring electricity back."

"Why?" Faumba asked passionately. "Why did it all happen?"

Bolingo met her daughter's eyes, "No one knows, Faumba. That's the Great Mystery. Some people think it was Earth itself, that the planet decided humans had taken too much and needed to be...

reduced. Others think it was some force we don't understand, something beyond humans. There are even stories about something called 'artificial intelligence' that humans created just before The Transition, a kind of thinking machine, but those stories are unclear. Whatever the cause, the result was that the human population went from billions to millions. From thousands of Tribes to hundreds. Those of us who remain have learned to live differently."

She returned to her weeding, voice softening, "Mdogo wangu, we have learned to live with what the earth provides, to not take more than we need. We have learned to value each human life because there are so few of us. We have learned to work together because we must, or else we will disappear."

Faumba looked down at the soil beneath her small hands, at the viridian plants pushing up and up and up toward the sky.

* * *

In her seventh Seasonal Cycle, Faumba's lessons expanded.

She learned to read and write in the elegant script that had evolved since The Transition, when the oldest surviving books from Before began crumbling and new methods of language and history preservation had to be developed. She learned mathematics. Addition, subtraction, and the basics of geometry that would later help understand trajectory and distance. She learned the names of plants and animals, which were edible and which were poison, which indicated clean water and which indicated danger.

Communication class was her favorite.

In mathematics, there were right and wrong answers.

In Communication, there were only honest answers and dishonest ones, clear expressions and muddy ones.

The Teacher for Communication was a man named Jabari, who had spent five Seasonal Cycles as a Contemplative in the Thinking

75

House before returning to teach. His gentle way of speaking housed even the most uncomfortable topics in the feeling of safety.

"Today wanafunzi," Teacher Jabari said one afternoon, "we're going to talk about desire."

The twelve children in the classroom exchanged glances. Faumba felt a flutter of nervousness in her stomach.

"Desire," Teacher Jabari continued, "is wanting something. It might be wanting food when you're hungry, or wanting to run when you've been sitting still too long, or wanting to be close to someone you care about. Desires are natural. They're part of being human.

"If any of you decide to follow the Contemplative path, you'll learn how desire and suffering are connected. For now, we will learn to recognize desires, to understand them, and to communicate them clearly to others. This is true for all desires, including the desires related to our bodies and intimacy with others."

The sentiment settled.

"Before The Transition, many Tribes taught that some desires, especially desires related to bodies and intimacy, were shameful, that they should be hidden or denied. This had many negative impacts. People felt broken for feeling natural things. They couldn't talk honestly with their partners. They made choices that hurt themselves and others because they never learned to understand what they truly wanted or needed."

Faumba thought of her mothers, how openly affectionate they were with each other, how they held hands while walking through the Village, how they kissed each other lovingly.

"After The Transition," Teacher Jabari went on, "humanity had to rebuild itself. We chose to rebuild differently. We chose to teach you, our children, that your body belongs to you. That your desires, whatever they are, are worth understanding. That you have the right to say yes to experiences that bring you joy, and no to ones that don't. And most importantly, that you can talk about all of this openly, without fear."

"This is just the beginning," he smiled at the children's serious faces. "Over many Seasonal Cycles, through Youth School, Adolescent School, and Higher School, you'll continue learning about yourself, about others, and about how to build relationships based on honesty and respect. Some of these lessons will feel awkward at first. This is okay. The awkwardness passes. The wisdom remains."

* * *

In her eighth Seasonal Cycle, Faumba began accompanying Esengo in the Workshop, an enormous structure near the center of their Team's complex. The Workshop was filled with a wide array tools and materials, with Artisans and Arrowsmiths and Carpenters all working side by side. The smell of wood shavings and stone dust swirled around the laboring. The sound of carving and sanding and hammering created a constant-t-t-t-t rhythm.

Esengo led Faumba to her workstation, where she'd been creating a series of small ceremonial bowls from mahogany, inlaying them with patterns of aquamarine and garnet.

"Tazama, my little rainbow, watch."

Faumba observed her mother's hands move with absolute precision, gouging tiny channels in the wood, fitting the gems into place, polishing the surface until it gleamed. Each bowl took several days to complete.

"Why do you make them so carefully?"

Faumba asked.

"Wouldn't it be faster to make them simpler?"

A smile played at the corners of Esengo lips.

"Faster, yes. But, would they be as beautiful? Would they last as long? Would they bring as much joy to the person who uses them?"

She set down her tools and gestured for Faumba to sit beside her.

"Before The Transition, humans made things very quickly. They had machines powered by electricity that could produce hundreds of objects in the time it takes me to make one bowl. Because they could make so many things so quickly, they didn't value them. They would use something once and throw it away. They would buy something new instead of repairing something old. They created mountains of waste, taking more resources from the earth than could be replaced."

Esengo picked up one of her completed bowls, running her fingers over its stone-studded surface.

"We live differently now. Not because we're better people, but because we have no choice. Without electricity, without machines, we can only make things slowly, with our hands. And so, we've learned to make things that last. To repair instead of replace. To value craftsmanship. To take only what we need with gratitude."

Handing the bowl to Faumba, "This will outlive me, possibly you too. Someone will use it for ceremonies, for special meals, for marking important moments in their life. They will pass it on to someone else, who will pass it on again, na kadhalika. One bowl, made with care, will serve the community for generations. That's worth the time it takes."

Faumba held the bowl carefully. She felt its weight, admiring the way the gems caught the light.

* * *

In her ninth Seasonal Cycle, Faumba visited the farmlands with Bolingo.

The expansive fields rolled toward the horizon, where the edge of Kinshasa Tribe met the dense rainforest. The bitter smell of dirt and compost was inescapable. Farmers tended to cassava and yams, plantains and corn, cowpeas and bottle gourds.

"The land is alive, imejaa uhai."

Bolingo was kneeling in the earth, running her fingers through the soil.

"Before The Transition, humans treated land like a machine, only useful for its output. They poured toxic fertilizer on the land to produce more and faster, not caring about the effects on health. They grew the same crop every Seasonal Cycle until the soil was exhausted. When that soil was dead, they simply moved on to new land and started the process again."

She brushed the dirt from her knees and stood, "Then The Transition came, and much of the land died. We don't know exactly why. Maybe humans pushed the earth too far, or some other force intervened."

Bolingo gestured to the fields around them, "We learned from our ancestors' mistakes. We plant what the land can support. We give back. We rest the fields regularly. We work with the earth's rhythms, instead of against them."

Smiling at her daughter, "Your generation will continue this wisdom. Traders tell us that some Tribes are experiencing food shortages because their land is beginning to fail. We don't know if this is because they're not farming sustainably, or if another shift is happening. This will be your challenge to navigate."

Faumba's sight stretched across the scene.

She watched the Farmers in communion with the land.

"Is it true," she asked, "that the weather has been changing? I heard some adults talking about it."

Bolingo's expression grew thoughtful, "Yes... in the last few Seasonal Cycles, the weather patterns have started to stabilize. During The Transition, the weather became chaotic. There were droughts in places that used to have rain, floods in places that used to be dry, massive storms that grew rapidly. But recently, things have been settling into more predictable patterns. We don't know what it means, whether it's good or bad, whether it will continue or reverse again. But we watch carefully and adapt."

With care, she placed her hand on Faumba's shoulder, "This is what I want you to understand, little rainbow. We live in a world of mysteries. We don't have all the answers. We will never have all the answers. But we keep observing and learning, doing our best to live in harmony with forces we don't fully understand."

\* \* \*

In her tenth Seasonal Cycle, Faumba received the first official lesson about The Transition in Youth School.

She'd heard fragments of the story from her mothers, from older children, from bits and pieces of adult conversation. She was brimming with anticipation for the official teaching, the organized sequence every child in every Tribe learned at this age.

The Teacher was a boy named Makambo.

At only thirteen Seasonal Cycles, he was already teaching. His grasp of complex ideas and ability to explain them clearly, convinced the Kinshasa Tribe Council to give young Makambo responsibility beyond his age.

Faumba was immediately intrigued. His head was shaved, unusual for someone so young. His voice, though yet to deepen fully, already carried a confidence beyond his years. His eyes held a restless wandering.

"Karibuni everyone, welcome. Jina langu ni Makambo," he introduced himself after the classes' Grounding.

"Today is a very special day. Today, you begin learning the full history of The Transition."

He reached for a cord next to the wall and pulled, revealing a large map of Earth that had clearly survived from Before. The smell of aged paper wafted through the room. The continents were still recognizable through the faded colors. Scattered across the map were dots of various colors, added more recently.

"This is our world," Makambo said. "Each dot represents a Tribe that exists today. Can you find the Tribe of Kinshasa?"

The children leaned forward, searching.

Faumba's eyes landed on a purple dot in the heart of the African continent.

"There," she pointed.

"Excellent, you notice well."

She smiled at the recognition.

Continuing, "According to our best information from Traders, there are about two hundred Tribes worldwide. But there used to be many more. Researchers estimate that before The Transition, there were about 1,500 Tribes. They were called cities then, spread across the planet. The global human population was measured in billions, not millions."

The enormous number sank in.

"About three hundred and fifty Seasonal Cycles ago, around Seasonal Cycle 2025, everything began to change."

He tugged another cord, revealing a second map clearly made after The Transition on rough pulp paper with muted red and brown pigments. It showed four drawings of the African continent labeled 2025, 2100, 2200, 2350.

"The Great Mystery reshaped the world in three ways," Makambo voice took on a storyteller's cadence.

"The first was land."

He pointed to the first image, representing viable farmland throughout the continent. Then the second, where vast areas had gone barren. Then the third and fourth, where smaller and smaller areas of fertile land were represented. The markings between fertile and infertile land were eerily straight.

"Without warning, fields that had fed thousands suddenly produced nothing. Farmers tried everything. Different seeds, different farming techniques, prayers to different gods. Nothing worked. And the pattern of failure..." tracing his finger along the straight lines, "notice how geometric it is. How precise. This couldn't have been disease or drought or natural degradation. This was something else.

"As you can imagine, this caused terrible suffering. Food became scarce. People starved. Conflicts broke out over the remaining resources. And the strange thing, the truly mysterious detail of it all, was that the pattern of land death seemed designed to funnel the surviving humans into specific areas, as if some force was deciding where humans could and couldn't live."

He paused, scanning the students' faces.

They were rapt with attention.

"The second mystery was fertility. Imagine a world where every woman could have children. Not just a few, but nearly everyone. That was the world Before. Women could decide when to have a child, and they usually could. They could have one, or two, or five, or even more."

The students' eyes widened at the incomprehensible.

He went on, "Then, around the same time the land began to die, women began to lose the ability to bear children. Not all women, but most. The few who retained fertility, the ones we now call Childbearers, all had something in common. They came from families with long histories of health and longevity. They had strong bodies and sharp minds. It was as though someone was selecting the healthiest humans to continue the species."

He wandered throughout the room, "This is why we are each precious, why our parents had to petition the Council for permission to raise us, why they had to take extensive training on how to raise us properly."

Faumba thought of the loving care her mothers poured into raising her, reframing with a new appreciation.

"The third mystery," Makambo said, returning to the front of the class, "was electricity.

"Imagine incredibly tiny particles, so small you can't see them. When these particles move together, they create electricity. Imagine electricity like the wind. You can't see it, but you can feel what it

82

does. Wind isn't stored in the air, wind moves through the air. Electricity is similar, moving through invisible charged particles.

"Before The Transition, humans had learned to harness this energy and make it flow through wires, long and thin pieces of metal. With this electricity, they could create light in the darkest night, preserve food for long periods, communicate across immense distances, and power machines that helped them farm, build, travel, heal. Life was very different."

His voice dropped, "Then one day, electricity simply stopped. All at once, everywhere in the world. The lights went dark. The machines went silent. And despite three hundred and fifty Seasonal Cycles of trying, despite studying every document we have from Before about how electricity worked, we have never been able to bring it back."

The classroom was completely silent.

"Some think," Makambo continued, "that the disappearance of electricity was connected to the other two mysteries. That they all had the same cause.

"There's one more piece to this puzzle. We know very little about, but it appears in documents from just before The Transition."

After pausing for dramatic effect, "In the final Seasonal Cycles before electricity vanished, humans had created something called 'artificial intelligence.' From what we can understand from record fragments, this was a kind of thinking machine. Imagine electricity so advanced and refined that it could make decisions like a human. It could learn, plan, and act on its own intentions."

Faumba felt a chill run down her spine.

"When electricity disappeared, so did artificial intelligence. We don't know if it was destroyed, or if it just left. The documents are unclear. Many scholars wonder if there's a connection, if perhaps this artificial intelligence had something to do with The Transition itself. Others think AI might still exist somehow, hiding, watching, waiting."

He straightened himself and took on the formal tone from before, "These are the mysteries we inherit. The questions our generation must continue to explore. We know what happened, but we don't know why, or how, or what it means for our future. All we know is that humanity survived and adapted, learning to live within the planet's limits."

He smiled gently at their serious faces, "For nearly two hundred and fifty Seasonal Cycles, our global population has remained stable at around one hundred million. We've learned to value cooperation over competition, sustainability over extraction, quality over quantity. We've learned these lessons because we had no choice."

Faumba walked home with her mind spinning. She'd known the broad outlines of The Transition, but hearing it laid out so completely, so systematically, made it feel more real, more unsettling.

* * *

The Seasonal Cycles passed.

Faumba continued her Communication lessons, growing more comfortable discussing desires, boundaries, and consent. She learned that attraction could take many forms, that some people were drawn to masculine energy, others to feminine energy, others to both or neither. She learned that some people experienced physical desire intensely and others hardly at all. She learned that Groupings could be two people or ten, could last a lifetime or a few Seasonal Cycles, and that they could be structured in infinite ways as long as everyone involved communicated honestly.

She experimented. A brief connection with a girl from another Team, a longer relationship with a boy named Kofi, a brief Grouping of three. Each taught her more about what she wanted, what she didn't, how to speak clearly about both.

She discovered that she was drawn primarily to masculine energy, though she appreciated beauty in all its forms. She learned that although she enjoyed physical intimacy, it wasn't central to her identity. She valued depth, favoring one deep connection over many shallow ones.

She sometimes saw Makambo venturing through the Village. She noticed the way people listened when he spoke with those far-seeing eyes.

* * *

By her eighteenth Seasonal Cycle, Faumba began Hunter training.

The role came naturally. She'd developed the quiet observation required to track animals, and the patience and precision for archery.

Faumba excelled rapidly, astonishing everyone. The skills required of a Hunter came with ease, mastering the abilities of reading the forest, moving silently, and steadying her breathing to release an arrow at the precise moment.

"I've never seen anything like it," one of the senior Hunters complimented after she pierced a giant forest hog from an impossible distance. "Are you even human?"

* * *

At twenty, Faumba attended the Annual Kinshasa Tribal Meeting for the first time as an adult. For three days, all one thousand Teams of Kinshasa Tribe gathered to share food, music, stories, and decisions.

Amidst the nighttime activity, Faumba turned to find herself face to face with Makambo.

He'd grown into full adulthood. He was taller than she remembered, with broad shoulders. His shaved head accentuated his feature's sharp intelligence. He wore a bright multi-colored cloth around his waist. Faumba's eyes outlined his body, as the firelight of a nearby torch bounced off his muscular frame.

She caught herself and met his eyes.

He was smiling.

"Habari yako Faumba? I heard you've become quite the Hunter."

She did her best not to blush, "Salama, asante. I heard you've become quite the researcher."

"Among other things," his smile widened. "Say, are you up to anything right now?

"Not really, just enjoying the Meeting," she attempted to not reveal her attraction.

"I was going to find some quiet, would you care to join?

She nodded enthusiastically.

They distanced from the noise to the quiet periphery. The night was warm, heavy with the scent of spices. They walked with a gentle, unhurried stride.

"I remember you," Makambo said. "From that class about The Transition. You were very attentive."

Faumba laughed, "You seemed ancient to me then, so confident and knowledgeable."

"I was terrified," he admitted, "Afraid I'd make a mistake, afraid the students would realize I was just a child myself playing at being a Teacher."

"You never showed it."

"Many thanks to the control of mind and emotions acquired through Grounding."

He added, "I've thought about you over the years, wondering what you'd become. I'm not surprised you're a Hunter. You had those qualities even back then. That stillness, that ability for deep observation."

Faumba felt warmth flare through her body, "Asanta bana. I've seen you around the Village. I've wanted to talk to you but, I didn't know if you'd remember me."

"Of course I remembered you." He took a small step forward, "You were the one who really wanted to understand."

They looked at each other in the dim light.

"I'm feeling something, but I'm not sure exactly what it is," Faumba fell back on her Communication training. "It's attraction, or curiosity, maybe something else. But I'd like to find out."

"As would I."

They shared stories and laughter until sunrise.

* * *

Over the following Seasonal Cycles, Faumba and Makambo built their relationship with attentive care.

They learned each other's rhythms. Faumba rising before dawn to hunt, Makambo staying up late poring over medical documents. They learned each other's desires, which type of touch meant yes and which meant no or not now. They learned to communicate with the language of familiarity.

They explored the full spectrum of intimacy post-Transition culture encouraged. They tried bringing a third person into their Grouping for a time, a man named Lokonga who they both cared for deeply, eventually recognizing they preferred the simplicity of two.

Faumba remembered how different this was from Before. How shame enveloped desires, unclear communication, relationships built on unspoken expectations and resentment.

Faumba experienced none of that. Everything was open, discussed, amplifying the magic.

* * *

By her twenty-third Seasonal Cycle, Faumba established herself as the most accomplished Hunter Kinshasa Tribe had ever known.

She could track a hog through the densest underbrush by the faintest traces. A bent leaf, a disturbed stone, the waft of a creature's musk, the subtle change in birdsong indicating an animal's passage. She could estimate the exact trajectory needed to arc an arrow through three layers of foliage and strike her target precisely between the eyes. She could read weather patterns in the sky and animal behavior in the forest to predict where prey would be hours before it arrived.

Other Hunters sought her training. Surrounding Villages requested her assistance. People began to speak of her with admiration and sentiments bordering awe.

"You're going to be nominated for Council," Makambo predicted one evening as they lay in bed.

Faumba groaned, "I know. I'm going to decline."

"Why?" He propped himself up to look at her, "You'd be brilliant on the Council. Everyone respects you. You could help guide policy on resource management, on inter-Tribal relations..."

"I don't want to spend my time in meetings," Faumba interrupted gently. "I want to spend it in the forest. I want to witness sunrises from the canopy. I want to feel the earth beneath my bare feet. That's where I belong, not in the Meeting Place."

Makambo then smiled. "You know, that's what I love most about you. You know exactly who you are."

"Do I?"

* * *

Now, at twenty-five Seasonal Cycles, Faumba found herself walking hand-in-hand with Makambo toward the Mayele Learning Center. As they climbed the spiral staircase of the Youth School tower, Faumba noticed the light that shined from everywhere.

# Chapter 16

A cascading sunrise illuminated the Tribe of Kinshasa with a tangible pulse. Every one of its five hundred thousand citizens awoke with anticipation. Two weeks had passed since Makambo's lesson. Two weeks remained until the 50th West African Regional Council Meeting would begin.

Travelers from distant Tribes had already set out, some journeying over one hundred days to witness and participate. Members from the Tribe of Lagos were well on their way to Kinshasa, alongside delegations from as far as Johannesburg Tribe and the Tribe of the Pyramids.

The Tribes of Lagos and Kinshasa alternated hosting the West African Regional Council Meeting every five Seasonal Cycles. With this gathering as their 50th assembly, preparations were more elaborate than ever.

These inter-Tribal events had woven themselves into the planet's new tapestry. Across the globe, Regional Council Meetings emerged wherever trade routes linked two or more Tribes. In contrast to the smaller Annual Tribal Council Meetings held within each Tribe, the Regional gatherings were immense ten-day affairs. Occasionally, urgent crises warranted an Emergency Regional Council Meeting.

For the West African Regional Council Meeting, Council Members from Lagos Tribe and Kinshasa Tribe would meet, as would representatives from smaller Villages and Teams throughout the region. Although living outside the structure of a Tribe was uncommon, scattered enclaves still dotted the globe. During these ten days, the Tribe of Kinshasa transformed itself into a radiant festival, celebrating diplomacy and culture on a monumental scale.

Over the centuries, each Tribe had refined a distinctive form of artistry. Lagos was celebrated for its vibrant music. Afrobeat, a fusion of pre-Transition jazz and highlife native to the region, had traveled through time, morphing and evolving, retaining the hypnotic rhythms of its ancestry. Whenever the Tribe of Lagos hosted the Regional meeting, musicians from across the continent gathered for a mesmerizing convergence of sound.

Kinshasa Tribe had earned renown through artistic installations, culminating in towering structures designed to dazzle and interact with visitors. Artisans worked tirelessly across the five Seasonal Cycles between Regional Council Meetings to develop feats of wooden engineering. Labyrinthine towers and interactive sculptures were designed and constructed for each event. This Seasonal Cycle, Kinshasa's Artisans created vertical mazes that required participants to solve puzzles en route to the exit. As a gesture of camaraderie, Lagosian Artisans were also invited to contribute installations throughout Kinshasa Tribe. In homage to the rainforest's bounty, everything was constructed from local mahogany, ebony, iroko, and wenge trees.

The wooden sculptures would be ritually burned at the end of the ten-day festival in recognition of impermanence's omnipresence. Onlookers watched in reverent silence as lights from the inferno dissolved into scintillations.

Not all affairs of the Meeting were purely celebratory. The Regional Council Meeting served the pragmatic function of addressing shared concerns and renegotiating trade agreements.

In the last five Seasonal Cycles, Kinshasa Tribe's Hunters had noticed a downturn in forest hog populations. This troubling scarcity was mirrored by Lagos Tribe's vanishing duikers, cane rats, and mona monkeys, as well as fish in local and coastal waterways. As game became harder to find, hunting expeditions stretched longer, feeding anxieties about resource depletion.

Other topics for debate ranged from adjusting trade tariffs to sharing the latest findings on malaria research that each Tribe had been conducting independently.

In this maelstrom of festivities and negotiations, Makambo's skilled artisanship positioned him as a valuable advisor. His insights guided teams testing mechanical features and refining adornments to ensure participants' marvel.

Immersed in these preparations, he spent his days in the Workshop alongside Esengo, shaping ebony arrowheads for an installation chronicling Kinshasa Tribe's legacy of giant forest hog hunting.

After a long and productive day, he headed home with the lengthening shadows.

"Welcome home, mwanga wangu," greeted Faumbe with affection radiating. "I brought back food from The Eatery earlier. Would you like me to heat it for you?"

"Faumba," with a voice full of fatigue, "I am the luckiest being alive. Asante sana. Yes, I'd love a warm meal."

She smiled, pressing a gentle kiss to his forehead. She kindled a fire in the stove made of salvaged metal. The food warmed slowly in a ceramic dish.

"How are the preparations coming?" Faumba asked, stirring the flames. "You're working on the Hunter Homage structure, sio?"

Makambo nodded. "That's the one, located on the other side of the Tribe. I must have passed fourteen Teams just to get there. The build is nearly finished, I think we'll finalize it tomorrow. I made one hundred seventy-four ebony arrowheads today." Flexing his fingers with a grimace, "My hands are aching."

91

Suddenly, a firm knock sounded at the door. They exchanged puzzled curiosity. Neither expected visitors, especially not so close to the Regional Council Meeting, when everyone was either buried in preparations or collapsed in rest.

Makambo rose to the door, sliding aside the small rectangular viewport. In a Team of roughly five hundred, everyone knew everyone. The face outside was unfamiliar.

"Habari? Who might you be?"

"Greetings," came the reply, courteous and direct. "Please pardon the intrusion. I am Bomoyi, a Messenger from the Tribal Council. I have a summons for both Faumba and Makambo."

"Karibu rafiki, please come in."

Makambo opened the door and offered the local gesture of welcome with his hands. Messengers, along with others occupying behind-the-scenes roles for the Tribe's Councils, were greatly respected.

Bomoyi's appearance was androgynous. Their eyes, lips, cheeks, chin, and shoulders did not comment on their biological sex. The cloth they wore was customarily worn by males, though their jewelry was customarily worn by women. Gender non-conforming beings such as Bomoyi were common throughout the globe in the post-Transition era.

"May I offer you some hibiscus tea?" Makambo asked politely.

"Asante, but I must decline," Bomoyi said briskly. "I have several summons to deliver tonight, so my visit must be brief."

"Hakuna shida," Makambo said. "Please, at least take a seat for a moment and catch your breath."

Bomoyi thanked him and settled into a nearby chair, joining Faumba and Makambo. Bomoyi retrieved two pieces of pulp paper from a satchel of woven raffia palm leaves. Bomoyi handed a slip of paper to both Faumba and Makambo.

Each paper had several lines of concise letters and symbols sketched in ornate handwriting:

"Your presence is formally requested at the 50th West African Regional Council hosted by the Tribe of Kinshasa. You are to appear before the Council on the 3rd day of the Meeting."

Noticing their notes bore the same message, they glanced at each other with questioning expressions.

The summons itself was not cause for alarm, as unexpected as it was. The first two days of the Regional Council Meeting were exclusively for seated Council Members from across the region. Beginning on the third day, select non-council members, those whose expertise or reputations warranted further consultation, were invited to appear.

Though crime was nearly absent from post-Transition life, there were still instances when one would succumb so deeply to emotion. The infractions so egregious they warranted Regional Council attention were addressed on the ninth day. The tenth day of the Regional Council Meetings was exclusively for celebration and merriment.

"I'm honored," Faumba stated after an interval of stillness, "but I can't quite see the reason. Any thoughts, Makambo?"

Makambo shook his head with a furrowed brow.

Bomoyi leaned forward, "I'm afraid I don't know the specifics." Standing and tucking their satchel beneath an arm, "I must continue, there are many more summons to deliver. Thank you for your hospitality. I wish you many blessings."

Bomoyi left the dwelling, disappearing into the twilight. Their footsteps merged with the bustle of toiling preparations.

## Chapter 17

The Tribe of Kinshasa found itself fully immersed in the vibrancy of the 50th West African Regional Council Meeting's third day. Loosened by the first two days settling in, participants struck up conversations with strangers, forging new bonds between the near and far.

Many visitors lodged in towering buildings, retrofitted from Before to serve as guest residences, displaying intricate carvings along the wooden reinforcements. A typical courtesy at Regional Council Meetings saw members of the host Tribe extend invitations for visitors to lodge in their own homes across the various Teams, offering a more personal and intimate glimpse into the host Tribe's way of life.

Of those who had traveled from the Tribe of Lagos was Yewándé, beloved companion and former lover of Faumba and Makambo. The three had once formed a low-commitment Grouping.

Originally from Lagos Tribe, Yewándé had moved to Kinshasa Tribe as a toddler where she was raised, attended School, and developed into her Role. Several Seasonal Cycles ago, Yewándé left Kinshasa to answer a summons from Lagos Tribe, which had admired her exceptional carpentry skills enough to request her permanent residence.

Of the three, Yewándé's complexion was the darkest shade of brown, extending to her closely shaven head. Her facial features were boldly defined, with full lips and piercing eyes. She ornamented her nose and ears with large piercings, emphasizing the graceful curves of her cheeks.

During the previous Regional Council Meeting, held by Lagos Tribe, Yewándé and a team of artisans had constructed an immense installation in honor of Lagos's fishing heritage. The sculpture sported an elaborate design portraying three Fishers in a boat, hoisting a life-sized, two-meter tarpon. Though primarily decorative, the boat's design fascinated the Carpenters of Lagos Tribe, who had been refining boat schematics for generations. Curiosity led them to replicate Yewándé's design, and to an astonished discovery that the resulting vessel outperformed all previous models in speed and stability.

Impressed by her inventive genius, the Lagos Tribal Council requested that the Kinshasa Tribal Council permit her formal relocation, reasoning that if Yewándé had devised such an extraordinary blueprint for decoration, what further innovations might she achieve when dedicated wholly to function and efficiency?

With the 50th West African Regional Council Meeting underway, Yewándé had arrived several days early to assist in building Lagos Tribe's installation celebrating cross-tribal collaboration. When those preparations finalized, she spent much of the opening days reveling in old friendships. Late-night dancing, sumptuous foods prepared exclusively for the Council Meeting, and the sensual warmth of the bedroom all played a part in welcoming her back to Kinshasa Tribe.

This third morning was given over to careful preparation for Faumba and Makambo's appearance before the Regional Council.

"Faumba, mrembo, have you seen my special necklace?" Makambo sifted through his jewelry box.

"The one with the tourmaline hog's head? It's right here." Faumba handed him the polished pink-and-green pendant which matched the ear and nose piercings he himself had made, reserved for the most ceremonious occasions.

Reclined on the bed, still unclothed from the previous night's revelry, Yewándé observed the interplay. "You two are so sweet together. I love watching your love," she noted with a playful smile.

Makambo looked up from fastening the necklace with a grin, "That's very kind of you, thank you. How is the health of your relationship these days?"

"Ayọ̀délé and I are so happy," Yewándé replied with pride. "Our home feels like a beacon of joy. In fact, when our Tribal Council approves our parenting request, we plan to begin the process with a Childbearer. We've been thinking about it for quite some time and couldn't be more thrilled."

Faumba gasped with excitement, "Yewándé! That's wonderful news. Why haven't you told us?"

"I was waiting for the perfect moment," Yewándé said with a broad grin.

Makambo, slipping on his formal robe, "Have you discussed any potential names?"

"We've toyed with a few ideas, but we're trying not to get too far ahead. Everyone knows that requesting a child doesn't always guarantee approval. But..." Her eyes sparkled, "We're thinking of Babatúndé, in honor of my grandfather, who transitioned to the Beyond recently. It's a Yoruba name traditionally given to a male child after losing an elder male. I thought that, since I'm now a member of the Tribe of Lagos again, and Ayọ̀délé's family has been there for many generations, it only makes sense to work towards understanding their culture more profoundly."

"That's a beautiful name," Faumba commented, seating herself next to Yewándé on the bed. "If the Lagos Tribal Council blesses you with a child, they'll be lucky to have you as a parent."

"Asante, Faumba," Yewándé said, leaning in for a soft kiss. Their lips lingered.

Their eyebrows softened.

The passion was propagating...

...until Makambo cleared his throat playfully.

"Ladies, as appealing as it is to continue the intimate dance, we can't afford to be late for our summons. You know how severe the penalty can be if we're tardy to a Regional Council Meeting, especially after being formally summoned."

He bent over to kiss each of their cheeks, "Let's save it for tonight."

Faumba rose to reach for her formal robe. Crafted by the Weavers of Kinshasa Tribe, the off-white garment extended to her ankles, its long sleeves decorated with carefully set gemstones. At the center of her chest was an embroidered hog's head of multicolored threads dyed with pigments derived from rainforest plants. The back of the robe was decorated with an elaborate embroidered depiction of a bow and arrow.

Makambo's robe, nearly identical in its overall cut and color, exhibited symbols signifying his present status as both Medical Researcher and Instructor, as well as the Role of Artisan he once held.

Allowed full artistic freedom, Weavers infused each ceremonial piece with slight variations on the forest hog design, ensuring no two robes were ever precisely the same.

Yewándé admired the pair, "You look immaculate, truly two of the most striking beings I've ever encountered."

"But not quite complete," Yewándé added, rising from the bed. From her satchel, she retrieved a small pot of wet clay. "I brought this from Lagos. It's a tradition we've adopted from the eastern communities. May I?"

The couple nodded.

Yewándé dipped her fingers into the dark clay and began tracing intricate designs across Faumba's forehead and cheekbones. The cool earth felt grounding against her skin. When she finished with Faumba, she turned to Makambo, adorning his face with similar patterns.

"There," Yewándé said, stepping back to admire her work. "Now you're ready to appear before the Council."

"Asante, Yewándé," Faumba and Makambo said in near unison.

Pausing a moment, "Any idea how you'll pass the time while we're in the meeting?" Makambo asked, remembering that Regional Council Meetings were closed to the public.

"I have a few musician friends offering a midday performance. We traveled together from Lagos Tribe, I can't wait to hear their new compositions they're debuting today. After that, well, I'll likely wander around, make new friends, eat delicious food. Enjoy yourselves, remember how significant it is to be summoned before the Council. It's a momentous moment for you both, I couldn't be more proud. If all goes smoothly," she added with a mischievous glint, "There'll be a prize waiting this evening."

Faumba and Makambo shared a smile. They answered Yewándé's farewell with a gentle kiss each, then stepped out into the brightness of Kinshasa Tribe's bustling streets.

* * *

The Meeting Place stood on the other side of the Tribe, adjacent to the Workshop and the renovated towers serving as traveler residencies.

Under normal conditions, the walk from Faumba and Makambo's dwelling to The Meeting Place took half an hour. They planned for it to take three times as long today, intending to savor the maze of wonder that'd subsumed the Tribe.

The smell hit them first.

Everywhere, food.

Oil sizzling in enormous pans, plantains caramelizing over open flames, groundnut stews releasing their earthy richness into the air. The scent of roasting cassava mingled with smoked fish, with the sharp brightness of ginger and the warm sweetness of coconut. Spices from across the continent, berbere from the east, suya spice from the west, created an olfactory mantle so dense it was almost visible. Faumba's stomach growled.

They paused at a corner where a woman from another Tribe offered skewered meat glazed with a sauce Faumba didn't recognize. The woman smiled, explaining it was made from tamarind and honey. They accepted gratefully, the tangy-sweet flavor coating their tongues.

The Festival swirled around them. A thousand conversations in shared Swahili. Laughter. Drumbeats. Children shrieking, darting between adults' legs.

Musicians musiced everywhere. Some performed formally on stages, others simply for the joy of it along the streets.

They walked slowly, absorbing it all.

Midway through the trek, they encountered a towering sculpture that drew a crowd so dense they had to wait their turn to approach.

The figure stood three meters tall, carved from leadwood so dark it seemed to drink in light. Mami Wata. The water spirit whose mythology had survived The Transition, carried across centuries and continents by those who remembered.

Her serpentine lower body coiled upward, scales suggested by geometric patterns carved into the near-black wood. Bold triangles and diamonds caught attention with their precision. Around these patterns, intricate Zulu beadwork had been incorporated into the sculpture itself. Bright reds, yellows, blues, and whites creating a stunning contrast against the dark leadwood. The beads traced the curves of her form, emphasizing movement frozen in wood.

Her torso rose gracefully, arms extended as if embracing sky and sea simultaneously. One hand held a mirror, the other a comb, traditional symbols from the old stories. Her face was serene, knowing, eternal.

A placard at the base explained, "Mami Wata: Mother of Waters, Guardian of Abundance, Symbol of the Connection Between All Waters and All People. From the Tribe of Johannesburg, in Recognition of Our Shared Heritage."

"I've never seen her depicted quite like this," Makambo whispered.

"She's beautiful," Faumba replied. "The way they've captured movement in something so still…"

A woman standing nearby, clearly from Johannesburg Tribe judging by the geometric patterns painted on her arms, smiled at them, "Our lead sculptor spent two full Seasonal Cycles on her. The leadwood is from our sacred groves. We journeyed over one hundred days to bring her here. We're honored to share her with Kinshasa Tribe."

Faumba inclined her head respectfully, "We're honored to receive her. Asante sana."

They stood for another moment, absorbing the sculpture's presence. There was something about Mami Wata that felt particularly resonant today. A sense of protection, perhaps. Or continuity. A reminder that some things endured.

Eventually, they moved on, though Faumba found herself glancing back once more at the dark figure towering above the crowd.

It was midday when they finally reached The Meeting Place, as Bomoyi's summons had indicated.

The Ceremonial Fire burned at the entrance, its tall flames warming the atmosphere's anticipation. Since the earliest Regional Council Meetings, this fire had served as a representation of the event's fervor and unifying spirit.

Adjacent to and mimicking the fire was a troupe of Dancers, tirelessly performing in rotation. As soon as one Dancer succumbed to the percussion music's unrelenting rhythm, a fresh body stepped in to take their place. The Dancers' masks were carved from local woods, each design portraying the various industries and lines of work that sustained Kinshasa Tribe.

Fire Chiefs maintained a vigilant watch on the blaze, periodically replenishing the wood to preserve its radiance around the clock. On the final day of the Regional Meeting, after all other ceremonial structures had been consigned to their own burnings, the Ceremonial Fire was finally allowed to die.

After enjoying the movements of The Dancers, Faumba and Makambo stepped through the grand entrance of The Meeting Place. Inside, they witnessed lavish beauty. The Meeting Place was one of the few buildings not repurposed from the remains of Before. Its design completely reflected post-Transition aesthetics. The spacious, circular chamber was enriched with meticulous carvings and frescos chronicling key moments of the Tribe's history. Overhead, thick wooden beams supported the high ceiling. Soft illumination filtered through the central skylight, granting the room a sense of quiet reverence.

As with the Mayele School Complex, the center of the floor bore a lavish mosaic depicting a hog's head, exhibiting an artful assembly of forest-gathered gemstones and multiple varieties of wood, their brown hues merging into subtle, harmonious gradients.

On either side of the grand entrance stood two staircases. Along with others summoned to appear before the Council, Faumba and Makambo climbed one of these staircases to a vantage point overlooking the entire chamber. From this elevated platform, additional windows permitted even more daylight to flood the vast interior.

Suffused with radiance, the hall offered the newcomers an immediate recognition of the importance of their presence.

Neither Faumba nor Makambo had visited The Meeting Place in quite some time, given the distance from their dwelling and the fact that their daily dealings were far removed from the Council's decision-making activities. In the silence of mutual awe, they paused to absorb the edifice's grandeur, each detail confirming the solemn significance of this assembly.

"I'm very proud to be a part of this Tribe," Makambo whispered, well aware that too loud an utterance would echo across the chamber. "We've accomplished so much, especially since The Transition."

"I couldn't agree more," Faumba whispered back. "Though I've only traveled to Lagos Tribe, I don't think anywhere else could feel so special to me. I love that this is our home."

Before either could say more, a troupe of Council Musicians filed into the central atrium. Custom dictated that every session, whether morning or afternoon, would open with music composed by the Council Band. Being appointed as a Council Musician was a deep honor, requiring mastery of an instrument and decades of service, though occasionally a prodigy rose to join the elders.

The Council Band comprised some twenty musicians, playing a mixture of wind, string, and percussive instruments. Their process for composing music functioned as a collective endeavor, with each member embellishing the ensemble's compositions in a careful and respectfully orchestrated collaboration.

During the Regional Council Meetings, the Council Band's performances were sonic marvels, reserved strictly for the ears of those officially summoned to the proceedings. Each piece was performed only once throughout the entire Meeting. This ephemeral detail paralleled the impermanent quality of the artistic installations, as well as the passing wonder of the Ceremonial Fire burning just outside.

The piece performed at this moment, that Faumba and Makambo were fortunate enough to witness, was magnificent beyond words.

It commenced with an interplay of string instruments, each musician arpeggiating a snippet of melody that, in isolation, would likely have sounded like complete nonsense. Taken together, the fragments merged into a brilliantly woven counterpoint, subtly referencing the anthem of Kinshasa Tribe.

Meanwhile, the horns sustained elongated pads of harmony, building a progression that refused to loop or repeat. From musical scores that survived since The Transition, the Musicians understood that Before, songs tended to recycle sets of chords, repeating harmonic cycles. In the post-Transition era, the aim of musical composition was to break that cyclical format in favor of through-composed works. This approach reflected the desire for a unique, post-Transition human identity. For percussion, Council Musicians employed drums and mallet instruments alike, evoking the marimbas once known in pre-Transition times.

The entire performance lasted about an hour, with flowing surges of energy crafting a spiritual experience perfectly suited to introduce the next phase of the day's Meeting. As the final notes faded in the resonant chamber, the Council Musicians remained still, allowing the reverberations...

...to die...

...in complete...

...silence.

The moment the chamber became entirely quiet, the eldest member of the Council Band led the ensemble from the hall through a door behind them, disappearing into the hushed corridors of The Meeting Place.

## Chapter 18

At the far side of The Meeting Place's central atrium, an elevated semicircle of chairs awaited the Regional Council. The Council Announcer emerged from a door behind these seats, wearing a flowing white gown akin to those worn by Faumba and Makambo. The pendant around her neck featured the carved visage of a hog's head, fashioned from the tusk of a giant forest hog. A tall ceremonial hat, secured with a chin strap, signaled her rank.

She addressed the gathering from the Speaker's Podium with clear and commanding authority.

"Greetings everyone, to the afternoon session of the third day of the 50th West African Regional Council Meeting. Ndugu zangu, wageni waalikwa, nawashukuru kwa kuhudhuria. Karibuni. Kindly rise to welcome the Council Members representing the Tribes of Lagos and Kinshasa, along with representatives from our region's independent Villages."

A subdued shuffle ensued as the attendees stood. Through the door behind the seats came the procession of 125 dignitaries whose gowns created a slow-moving rainbow across the atrium. Each's unique adornment, with intricate embroidery, represented their life's journey and the Roles they had fulfilled. Weavers had diligently incorporated biographical elements into the swirling patterns, a process that could take an entire Seasonal Cycle to complete for each gown.

Faumba watched them enter. Their faces bore the unmistakable residue of deliberations already undertaken, and those yet to come.

Of their many adornments was a light blue braided rope hung around their necks, indicating the time they had spent as a Contemplative. A bright orange cord confirmed their completion of the annual cognitive exams ensuring their mental acuity for Council service.

The pendants shared  their origins. Similar to the Announcer, Kinshasa Tribe's Council Members wore tusk pendants depicting a hog's head, while those from Lagos displayed fish pendants sculpted from harvested aquatic bones. Independent representatives bore ornaments reflecting the flora or fauna of their home regions. Faumba found her eyes returning to the delegate from the Tribe of the Pyramids.

One by one, all 125 Council Members filed in: fifty from Kinshasa Tribe's Villages, fifty from Lagos Tribe's, twenty-four from the region's independent Villages, and the delegate from the Tribe of the Pyramids. A tableau of skill, heritage, and diverse experience of post-Transition history.

When each dignitary reached their designated seat, the Council Announcer once again took the Speaker's Podium. "Please welcome the Kinshasa Tribe Council Choir," she declared.

From the grand entrance marched a group of twenty singers, clad in their own ceremonial gowns. Their coordinated steps echoed softly through the atrium. While the earlier performance by the Council Band alluded to the Tribe's anthem, these vocalists presented it in its original, unabridged form. Their voices rose in unison:

"Kinshasa, soil beneath our feet,
Where our ancestors rest and rise.
Though The Transition reshaped our ways,
Each dawn's promise rekindles our souls..."

Lush harmonies rang through the domed chamber, saturating the room with a reverential sense of belonging and pride. Faumba felt the familiar swell of resilience.

The moment the final tone dissolved into silence, the choir turned and exited through the main doors, leaving a vibrant quiet in their wake. When the last member disappeared through the door, the Council Members settled into their seats.

"Tunawapongeza na kuwashukuru, kwaya. Without further ado," declared the Council Announcer, "we shall commence this afternoon's session.

"Citizens of both Kinshasa and Lagos Tribes have been summoned to appear before the Regional Council. Today's proceedings will open with the presentation of the first group. All those whose summons indicate membership in this group, please proceed to the floor."

Makambo belonged to this first group.

Faumba breathed deeply. She had known he would be called, his summons had said as much. But knowing and witnessing are different creatures.

Rising from his seat, he glanced back at her with a faint smile. His expression painted an amalgam of uncertain anticipation.

She tried to smile, managing something close.

As he descended to the atrium floor, he recognized many of the converging individuals as Medical Researchers with whom he had recently collaborated. Once assembled, they formed a semicircle around the hog's head mosaic set in the ground, turning to face the elevated seats where the Regional Council presided.

The Council Announcer yielded the Speaker's Podium to another Council Member. Draped in robes of midnight-black cloth, his embroidery proclaimed a storied professional life including a lengthy tenure as a Medical Researcher. At the gown's center shone an ornate depiction of a microscope.

"Greetings, esteemed members of both Kinshasa and Lagos Tribes, nawakaribisha nyote," the speaker began, unhurried. "I am Olúṣẹgun, Council Member from the Tribe of Kinshasa. You have been summoned today for your contributions in advancing our understanding of an illness that has long afflicted our people since before The Transition."

Olúṣẹgun's deliberate voice resonated throughout the voluminous chamber. Faumba knew the name. Everyone did. Renowned across the entire African Continent, he had earned acclaim for his research into malaria's regional effects. Many Seasonal Cycles before, Olúṣẹgun and a team of fellow Medical Researchers managed to rediscover a definitive means of diagnosing malaria. Ordinarily, one might suspect an infection from symptoms such as cyclical fever, chills, profuse sweating, marked fatigue, muscle aches, headache, nausea, vomiting, and loss of appetite. Yet these same indicators overlapped with dengue fever, typhoid fever, yellow fever, and a host of other ailments.

As the Seasonal Cycles following The Transition went on, those same feverish symptoms still appeared, yet fatalities became increasingly rare. Olúṣẹgun hypothesized that malaria, the most lethal of the diseases exhibiting these signs, was waning from the human experience. His team collected data from universities and research centers that once existed worldwide, collaborating with both Water and Land Traders. Through this extensive research, they discovered a new method for diagnosing malaria, one that required no electricity.

A pivotal revelation arose when they learned of a way to execute a Rapid Diagnostic Test without electrical power. Historical documents showed that pre-Transition Medical Researchers had relied on a Microscopic Blood Smear Test, which required use a microscope plus particular staining chemicals. The stars aligned when a caravan of Traders arrived in Kinshasa Tribe bearing crates of supplies sourced from Northern Abya Yala. Among these materials were the test strips, staining agents, and mirror-reflected microscopes, substitutes for their electric counterparts. Armed with these tools, Olúṣẹ́gun's team began systematically testing people who displayed the characteristic symptoms, ultimately confirming that incidents of malaria were indeed in decline.

This confirmation reshaped medical understanding across Central Africa. The deadliest of the old diseases was mysteriously loosening its grip.

"As many of you know," Olúṣẹ́gun continued, addressing the Medical Researchers on the floor, "a Land Trader uncovered documents amid the ruins of what was once Makerere University. These pre-Transition papers concerned malaria research of that era. For several decades, we've charted a steady reduction in malaria cases in and around Kinshasa Tribe. This is a remarkable trend, though one whose explanation has eluded us. These records may provide the missing link."

After a brief throat clearing, "It appears that, prior to The Transition, scientists were investigating the genetic condition Glucose-6-Phosphate Dehydrogenase Deficiency. G6PD deficiency. A deficiency of this particular enzyme relates directly to malaria resistance."

Faumba watched Makambo's shoulders shift. He was leaning forward slightly, the way he did when a problem began revealing its shape.

"We have today with us a Council Member representing the Tribe of the Pyramids," Olúṣẹ́gun said, gesturing, "to share what her people have discovered. Tafadhali karibuni, Isis."

The woman with the stone triangles rose.

She swayed to the podium with a grace that mimicked swirling sand, the movement mirrored by hair stretching to her ankles. Her eyes were pale against warm caramel skin, her robe the color of northern desert sands. The embroidery covering her gown depicted the geometric lattices of molecular structures that seemed to belong to another world.

"Greetings, members of Lagos and Kinshasa Tribes. Asante sana kwa kunialika." Her voice carried, "I am thankful for the chance to speak before you."

She nodded toward Olúṣẹ́gun, "Your historic achievements in malaria research have paved the way for this moment."

Turning to the Medical Researchers on the floor, "All of you, through your intellect and dedication, have advanced humanity's fight against maladies persisting since before The Transition. Now, we call upon your expertise once again."

Isis drew a breath as Faumba found herself holding her own.

"Al-Azhar University once stood in the Tribe of the Pyramids, home to an extraordinary library. Through the Seasonal Cycles since The Transition, our Researchers have studied the documents preserved there, hoping to rebuild the body of knowledge inherited from pre-Transition humanity.

"When the Medical Researchers of Kinshasa Tribe reviewed the papers from Makerere University, detailing G6PD deficiency and its link to malaria resistance, a Kinshasa Tribe Scribe diligently duplicated those papers. A Messenger delivered them to us in the north. Upon receiving them, we were astounded.

"Within those documents, we observed that Makerere University's scientists had detailed specific instructions for identifying G6PD deficiency. They referenced testing kits named Standard Diagnostics Biosensor kits, capable of performing these tests without electricity. In the aftermath of discovering these instructions, we searched for the kits. We could not locate them, until now."

Murmurs rippled through the researchers. Faumba saw Makambo exchange a glance with the colleague beside him.

"While poring over materials in Al-Azhar's extensive library," Isis continued, "we realized we had possessed those very kits all along. Our Medical Researchers had unearthed them many Seasonal Cycles ago, during excavations of structures buried under drifting sands. At the time, we had no clue as to what purpose they served. They lay dormant in storage, waiting for context to give them meaning."

With a knowing smile, "This means we can finally understand why malaria rates have declined here in Central Africa and endeavor to replicate the success elsewhere."

Faumba's racing mind was assembling the forthcoming.

"The workings of these testing kits are too elaborate to expound upon now," Isis said. "You'll receive instruction on your journey to the Tribe of the Pyramids."

The ground shifted beneath Faumba.

"Ndiyo," Isis confirmed, her gaze sweeping across the assembled researchers. "Your summons is to journey to the Tribe of the Pyramids, to advance our collective knowledge of G6PD deficiency and its role in curbing malaria. The trip is both extensive and demanding. Five thousand kilometers to the north. At a pace of twenty to forty kilometers per day, factoring in varied terrain, the trek will last an entire Seasonal Cycle just to arrive."

Faumba calculated without wanting to.

A Seasonal Cycle there.

The research time?

Another Seasonal Cycle? Two?

Then a Seasonal Cycle back.

Three Seasonal Cycles, at minimum.

"We remind you of the promise you made when you accepted your role as Medical Researchers," Isis said, her voice adopting a ceremonial gravity, "to dedicate your intellectual talents to the

welfare of all humanity. We thank you for that commitment, and assure you that, once your endeavors are complete, your contributions
shall be etched permanently into the annals of post-Transition history."

Makambo turned.

His eyes found Faumba's across the chamber, across the dignitaries, and across the weight of history being made. She saw a restless wandering in his eyes as hers glistened with tears.

# Chapter 19

Faumba and Makambo had scarcely begun to process the magnitude of the announcement when their mourning was interrupted. No sooner had Isis returned to her seat than Olúṣẹ́gun, moving with that slow deliberation, resumed the Speaker's Podium.

"Friends," he began. "We recognize this is weighty news. We have no wish to overwhelm you prematurely. Please, enjoy the remainder of the 50th West African Regional Council Meeting. Once the festivities conclude, you will attend a briefing session. A Council Messenger will be in contact. In the briefing session you will meet the other members of your team, including Traders from Kinshasa Tribe whose routes connect our territory to the Tribe of the Pyramids. Rest assured, you will be in capable hands. Asante kwa huduma yenu. You may return to your seats."

Makambo and the others walked back across the ornate mosaic floor, ascending the stairs to the seating area. They projected composure. Faumba's cheeks were damp with tears she hadn't managed to restrain.

When Makambo reached her, they embraced with profound tenderness. Their cheeks touched, feeling the truth of love in the soft pressure of skin against skin.

The moment was short-lived.

"Those in the second group of summons," the Council Announcer's voice filled The Meeting Place, "please make your way to the center of the atrium."

Faumba's turn.

She concluded the embrace with a delicate kiss, taking a moment to hold Makambo's eyes. They were being presented with another opportunity, perhaps the most challenging yet, to honor their commitment to support each other's growth.

Descending the steps, she observed a pattern. Just as Makambo had noticed Medical Researchers converging around him, she recognized the finest Hunters of Kinshasa Tribe making their way to the floor. Among them were notable Fishers from Lagos Tribe and beyond, renowned throughout the region for their prowess.

They formed a semicircle around the hog's head mosaic, facing the elevated Council seats. The Council Announcer stepped aside, yielding the podium to a new figure.

"Greetings, honored members of Kinshasa and Lagos Tribes, and representatives of our neighboring Villages." The speaker's intonation carried the same ceremonial weight as Olúṣẹ́gun's. "I am Fúnmilọlá, Council Member of Lagos Tribe. You are here today because of your vital contributions in sustaining your communities. You have shown exemplary expertise in tracking and securing food, techniques predating even The Transition. Now we call upon you again to assist in unraveling a disturbing mystery that has recently afflicted our entire region."

Fúnmilọlá's gown shone in pale blues, inspired by seasons spent fishing the open waters west of Lagos Tribe. Around their neck hung a pendant carved from fish bone depicting the great tarpon, the traditional signet of Lagos. The embroidery on their gown rendered a fluid net in dark blues and purples, looping gracefully around their arms and waist. Across their back spread an elaborate fish motif, caught in the net's delicate web.

"As you know from firsthand experience in our waters and forests, the populations of game animals have been waning. Your expeditions have grown longer. You have ventured farther to find what once was plentiful. In Kinshasa Tribe, giant forest hogs grow scarce. In Lagos Tribe, tarpons, tigerfish, and other marine life have similarly diminished.

"The mystery doesn't stop with wildlife. Crop yields on arable lands are also declining. We have conferred with regional Villages and confirmed this is not isolated to our Tribes. Among us today is Ngwefuni, Council Member from the Village of Yaoundé."

At the mention of their name, Ngwefuni rose, offered a slight bow, then returned to their seat.

"Since The Transition," Fúnmilǫ́lá continued, "the Village of Yaoundé has migrated northward until it reached the confluence of the Sanaga and Mbam rivers. Its people became adept navigators of these waterways, experts at Fishing. Through Ngwefuni's testimony, we have learned they face the same hardships in locating fish as we do. This threatens to reduce our capacity to grant Childbearing requests, potentially resulting in a drastic lowering of population numbers. We cannot allow The Transition to repeat itself."

The statement's weight permeated the chamber.

"We must understand what is happening to our land and waters. You in this circle are the finest Hunters and Fishers our region has ever produced."

Fúnmilǫ́lá's gaze found Faumba.

"I want to particularly recognize Faumba, whose renown as a Hunter has become legend across the continent."

Faumba allowed her stern composure to soften. A slight smile, a nod toward Fúnmilǫ́lá and the Council Members. In her peripheral vision, she noticed Makambo beaming.

"Faumba," Fúnmilǫ́lá continued, "your tracking abilities are unparalleled. Your Contemplative training has endowed you with exemplary poise. You are recognized for exceptional Communication skills. Your peers attest to your gift for clear, collected expression, and perhaps more importantly, your capacity for deeply attuned listening.

"For these reasons, the Regional Council has determined that you will lead the effort to unveil the mystery threatening our region."

Applause began among the Council Members, then spread through The Meeting Place. The chamber filled with overlapping celebration as late afternoon light spilled through the skylight above. Faumba's honed hearing picked out Makambo's clapping from the chorus. She smiled, absorbing the celebratory energy.

When the applause subsided, Fúnmilọ́lá's voice resumed, "You will use your tracking talents to determine where the game has gone, leaning on your survival acumen to withstand many days and nights in the wilderness. You will collaborate with Farmers from Lagos and Kinshasa Tribes, exploring possible connections between shrinking farmland and the disappearance of animals."

Sombering, "As history taught us, during The Transition, once-fertile soil began to die a seemingly calculated patterns. As much as we hope otherwise, we suspect the unknown force behind the Great Mystery may be re-emerging."

The chamber felt silent.

"Faumba, you and the Hunters and Fishers at your side are entrusted with a mission of utmost importance. Hundreds of thousands depend on you to unravel these new realities afflicting our homelands. A Council Messenger will provide additional instructions after the festivities conclude. May luck and favor be with you. You may return to your seats."

Faumba and the others slowly filed back. The shock was evident in their movements. When she arrived before Makambo, her cool and unreadable demeanor hid surges of excitement mixed with the weight of everything.

Makambo, still processing his own news, greeted her with an empathetic embrace. He sensed the conflict rippling through her.

115

Hand in hand, they settled into their seats. His thumb gently caressed her hand.

The rest of the afternoon blurred.

Two more groups appeared before the Council. One consisted of Head Food Preparers from both Tribes and outlying Villages, instructed to refine techniques so that whatever fish and game did arrive might sustain more people. Another was composed of Water and Land Traders from the West African region, tasked with exploring new paths toward the distant Far East.

Faumba and Makambo scarcely paid attention. He rested his head on her shoulder. An occasional tear revealed the impact on their internal landscapes.

# Chapter 20

The Tribe of Kinshasa had resumed its typical rhythms in the month that had passed since the 10th day of the 50th West African Regional Council Meeting.

The Meeting's concluding days had been dedicated to indulgence. The nights were alive with dancing and feasting. The artistic structures scattered throughout the Tribe's land met their end in ritual flames. The grand Ceremonial Fire in front of The Meeting Place burned itself out in regal fashion.

On the Meeting's final day, all who had been summoned for a special mission were officially honored. Yewándé had decorated Faumba and Makambo's faces again with intricate designs of wet clay. The Council Band and Council Choir performed a piece charged with solemnity and excitement as Olúṣẹ́gun announced the names of those departing to fulfill tasks vital to the region's future.

Each name was met with applause. Each recipient was presented with an embroidered bracelet featuring the Glossy Ibis, the migratory bird who'd always find its way back to Central Africa each Seasonal Cycle. The bracelet's colors of metallic green, rust red, and muted purple resembled the Ibis' feathers. Bowing before Olúṣẹ́gun, Faumba and Makambo stepped aside bowing to Fúnmilọ́lá, who secured the bracelets around their ankles, leaving their hands free for work.

When the final name was read and the Closing Ceremony concluded, every attendee turned to face the Ceremonial Fire. The assembly entered a collective meditation, watching the flames naturally subside into glowing embers of undulating hues, dimming into lifeless coals. Given the fire's formidable size, onlookers stood late into the night, witnessing this gradual descent. The surrounding festivities produced a soft clamor, a background soundtrack to the fire's vanishing light.

Their bodies ached from standing so long. This intentional discomfort formed a visceral reminder of the sorrow and hardship of The Transition, of the endurance humankind had mustered to march forward into the unknown.

Faumba and Makambo were scheduled to embark on their separate journeys on the same day.

Yewándé was with them in their dwelling the night before departing. She had extended her stay in Kinshasa Tribe to savor every last moment with her former lovers. She would return to Lagos Tribe later, trusting Ayọ̀délé would understand.

As the sun settled outside, Yewándé reclined on the bed, running through final preparations.

"Knife?"

"Got it," they answered in unison.

"Sun cap?"

"Got it."

"Water container?"

"Nimepata."

On and on, verifying every item.

Their training sessions outlined how long they might be gone. For Makambo, a Seasonal Cycle's trek north to the Tribe of the Pyramids was certain. Faumba's mission remained open-ended, traveling through rainforests and farmland between Kinshasa and Lagos Tribes, seeking answers to the mysterious depletions.

Their training had been long and dense with new information. Faumba's sessions were a mixture of cross-training with Hunters and Fishers from both Tribes. Farmers from across West Africa attended, sharing data on withering lands, though no conclusive explanation emerged. Sometimes they practiced in the rainforest, exchanging tracking methods. Other times, Farmers spoke of once-fertile soils going inexplicably fallow.

Neither "nervous" nor "excited" captured Faumba's feelings. "Curious" and "skeptical" were more apt. Her mind was already assembling hypotheses and forming strategies.

Makambo's training took a different shape. He spent the month at the Kinshasa Tribe Medical Research Center, an old edifice near The Meeting Place. The building's entrance showcased the tribe's hog's head emblem, amended slightly with a depiction of two open hands signifying service. Other service-oriented facilities throughout the Tribe of Kinshasa bore the same symbolic revision.

Medical Researchers from across the Tribe converged, piecing together pre-Transition knowledge scattered worldwide. Isis led the seminars. Formerly a Head Medical Researcher in the Tribe of the Pyramids, she now served in a consulting capacity, bridging the Makerere documents with the rediscovered Biosensor kits. Her clear and gentle communication allowed complete understanding of the task's nuances.

When Yewándé exhausted the final items on the packing list, Faumba and Makambo joined her on the bed. The sun had settled beyond the horizon. They would embark at sunrise. Candlelight danced on their dark brown skin as they relaxed into their last hours together.

"As much as I'll miss you both," Makambo murmured, breaking the calm, "I'm genuinely excited. The information from our training has my curiosity buzzing."

"Oh yeah?" Faumba's head rested on Yewándé's chest. "Tell us more."

"It's rather technical. Do I have consent to shift the energy with analytical talk?"

The question was standard practice. In Communication and Child Raising Classes, one learned how their actions might influence another's emotional and energetic states. This awareness shaped them into adults conscious of such subtleties. Recognizing that Faumba and Yewándé were presently at ease, Makambo took care not to thrust technical matters upon them prematurely.

"You have my consent," Faumba said, smiling.

"Mine too," Yewándé added.

"Asante," Makambo grinned, bowing his head slightly. "There's scientific terminology involved. May I assume you both retain a general understanding of biology from Higher School?"

Nodding and exchanging a look, they found his excitement adorable.

"Excellent!" Modulating his tone, "Well, the scrolls from Makerere contain far more detail than we first assumed."

He shifted forward on the bed.

"They describe precise methods for detecting glucose-6-phosphate dehydrogenase deficiency, G6PD, without electricity, using those Biosensor kits discovered in the Tribe of the Pyramids.

"You may be asking yourself, why does this matter? Well, G6PD is an enzyme that protects blood from oxidative stress. The Makerere papers discuss free radicals, unstable molecules associated with various diseases including malaria, which has plagued this land for centuries. Oxidative stress is even linked to cancer, for which there was no cure even before The Transition.

"In people with G6PD deficiency, the enzyme is absent or defective. Their blood cells are more likely to break down through hemolysis. Malaria is caused by Plasmodium parasites that infect blood cells, multiply, and cause rupture. The parasites produce free radicals that accelerate this process. In those with G6PD deficiency, the defective enzyme cannot protect red blood cells, making them more vulnerable."

His eyes were bright.

"Here's the paradox. While G6PD deficiency increases susceptibility to hemolysis, it also increases resistance to malaria infection!"

Makambo was nearly falling off the bed.

Yewándé continued caressing the back of Faumba's neck as they listened.

"The resistance occurs because the defective enzyme is less efficient at producing NADPH, a molecule the parasites need to grow and multiply. People with G6PD deficiency may have fewer parasites in their blood, making them less likely to develop severe malaria.

"During our training, we gained a broader understanding of Olúṣẹ́gun's research. We're coming to see that the decrease in malaria in our region is likely related to high prevalence of G6PD deficiency here in West Africa, due to selective pressure. Over generations, people with the trait survived malaria and passed it to their offspring. This led to increased frequency in our populations.

"The ability to definitively detect G6PD deficiency will be one of the most significant breakthroughs in understanding malarial resistance, even compared to research before The Transition!"

He exhaled, checking that he hadn't overwhelmed.

"My role in the Tribe of the Pyramids will be to master this technique. Malaria has impacted communities along the Mediterranean as well, so we'll collaborate with those populations first, streamline the process, then return to West Africa to implement it at scale."

Softening his tone, "This means I'll be gone at least three Seasonal Cycles. Most likely longer." His gaze fixed on Faumba. "Mrembo, I'm going to miss you more deeply than words can convey."

"And I you, Makambo." She smiled, but it didn't quite reach her eyes, "I know you're off to do important work, benefiting our Tribe and beyond. But that doesn't make this any easier."

Makambo eased back onto the bed, arranging so Faumba lay between him and Yewándé. The three shared prolonged silence, focusing on breath and each other's warmth.

Yewándé's voice broke the spell.

Excitedly, "I have an idea. Before coming to Kinshasa for the Regional Council Meeting, Ayòdélé and I had been exploring new tantra techniques."

Faumba and Makambo exchanged a look, amusement playing across their expressions.

"With your permission," Yewándé continued, "I would love to bask in intimate energy with you both, allowing our energies to create a vortex of pleasure. Who knows how many Seasonal Cycles until we see each other again, if ever. I would love one more round of bliss."

"I would be delighted to dance in the nuances of intimacy with you both," Faumba affirmed.

"As would I," Makambo added.

Yewándé smiled.

She shifted to her knees between them.

Slowly, she placed a tender kiss on Faumba's forehead, then Makambo's. She followed a mindful, sensual procession down their bodies. The candle aimed its spear of light toward nirvana, glowing softly upon the intimacy for her delicate movements.

# Chapter 21

The first rays of sunlight filtered through the interlaced palm fronds and broad banana leaves of Faumba's A-frame tent. This lightweight lodging, shown in the early days of Hunter training, was ideally suited for the rainy season.

She greeted the day with gentle stretches. Touching her toes. Bending backward. Extending her arms across her body.

Then her mindfulness routine, followed by a brief exercise regimen adapted to the small space.

Exiting, she encountered a scene becoming steadily familiar. Several branch-and-leaf structures arranged around a fire pit, itself sheltered beneath a canopy of foliage where the team had prepared a meal of bush rats the previous evening. Faint stirrings from the other shelters signaled her companions' gradual awakening.

Faumba's party was now in their third month of investigations. They had made camp in an area once known as Mbanza Ngungu, roughly 140 kilometers southwest of Kinshasa Tribe. Before The Transition, Mbanza Ngungu was about the size of ten Villages and had been abandoned many Seasonal Cycles ago. Remnants of steel-and-concrete buildings lined the streets in silent disrepair. The team took refuge in a green space toward the west, where a heavily rusted metal sign with the words "Cimetière Nsona-Nkulu" carved out still stood at the entrance.

Most of Faumba's current group consisted of Hunters from Kinshasa and Lagos Tribes, supplemented by a handful of Farmers. Early in the expedition, Fishers from both Tribes opted to remain along the waterways, splitting from the Hunters at Zongo Falls on the Inkisi River. They agreed to reconvene in another month at the Pioka section of the Congo River to compare findings.

The previous night, the team had designated Túndé, a Hunter from Lagos Tribe, to gather breakfast. By the time Faumba emerged, an assortment of mangoes, pineapples, and papayas lay beside the fire pit while Túndé stood over a modest blaze, preparing plantains and leftover bush rat.

She greeted him, settling at his side.

They dined in quiet comradery on voluptuously succulent fruit, savoring each sweet, dripping bite. Although farmland had been mysteriously diminishing, fruit-bearing trees continued to thrive, unscathed by whatever force was depleting arable land. Council Members in both Tribes remained keenly aware that fruit alone could not sustain entire populations, and any plan to cultivate it en masse would strip resources at an unsustainable rate.

Fourteen Hunters comprised this subset of the original expedition team. In keeping with the Council's directives, Faumba took charge, effortlessly proving her mettle as Kinshasa Tribe's finest tracker. When she finished her meal, she retrieved a map from her satchel.

The satchel was a gift from Yewándé. In the final month before departure, Yewándé had commissioned Leatherworkers to tan forest hog hide, crafting beautiful and reliable bags for both Faumba and Makambo. As Faumba spread the map on the ground, she momentarily thought of that last evening of intimacy.

"Good morning, everyone," she announced, standing so all could see. "I trust you slept well and enjoyed breakfast. Asante to Túndé for gathering and preparing this meal."

A chorus of thanks before she continued.

"We've reached a decisive juncture. While we still haven't pinpointed the forest hog populations, we found signs yesterday suggesting they've moved farther south. I've devised a plan. We'll fan out to explore surrounding areas for more tracks, regrouping here by nightfall to share findings. Each group should keep within ten to twenty kilometers, devoting our awareness to careful tracking. Pay attention to changes in local foliage or grasses that might indicate the hogs' preferred routes, or whatever's compelling them onward."

Surveyed the group and assigning tasks, "Túndé and I will head southeast. There's a cave system that's intriguing me." She knew her skills were adequate for a solo venture.

Yet, one of the most essential principles taught during Hunter training was never to overestimate one's capacity. Journeying in pairs mitigated against the unforeseen.

Another core tenet insisted on the primacy of instinct, as vital in the wilderness as analytical reasoning.

Pointing left, "You six, southwest."

Pointing right, "You six, directly south."

"Return when the clouds turn orange. Finish your meals quickly, and gather your gear. We leave in fifteen minutes. Don't stray too far. Focus on your tracking expertise, observe every subtlety."

Her instructions were succinct, almost cold. The team understood that certain circumstances demanded stark clarity.

Túndé approached with a confused look.

"Faumba, you mentioned a cave system. In all my training, giant forest hogs have always stuck to wet forests with heavy vegetation. Why explore a cave?"

"Túndé," she replied, confident but not condescending, "in unprecedented circumstances, you have to think creatively. If something mysterious is developing with the hogs' movement patterns, we can't expect to find answers using conventional approaches. Maybe they're evolving to prefer caves. If we haven't observed them in expected locations, perhaps they've developed a preference for secluded shelter."

His eyes flickered with respect, "No wonder the Regional Council chose you to lead."

Soon, the others emerged from their shelters with packed satchels. After a brief communal meditation, they split off in three directions.

Faumba and Túndé walked for several hours. Though the morning sun was not yet at its zenith, warmth and humidity pressed in, drenching their bodies with sweat. A change in the atmosphere's smell told of an incoming rainstorm.

Both traveled barefoot, methodically placing each step so as not to disturb their surroundings.

They were headed southwest toward Ngovo Cave. Faumba had visited the cave system many Seasonal Cycles ago during her earliest Hunter training. She recalled the impressive entrance draped in vines and cascading water, the network of passages leading to an underground waterfall, pools teeming with blind fish.

If I were a giant forest hog, she mused, Ngovo Cave would be ideal shelter.

"Faumba!" Túndé yelled, "Look!"

He had drifted several meters ahead.

She caught up.

With a gentle reproach, "Túndé, I understand you're excited, but raising our voices may startle the hogs. The last thing we want is to influence their movements. What is it?"

He gestured to a dense patch of undergrowth.

They had been surveying diligently for any sign of giant forest hog activity. This was no small feat, given these animals' propensity for deep vegetation.

Directly ahead lay one of the clearest indicators yet. Underbrush flattened in a way that hinted at a hog's preferred resting place. Nearby, a patch of wet mud offered unmistakable evidence of recent wallowing. The surrounding trees bore rub marks where hogs scratch after a muddy soak.

The prints and disturbed foliage suggested a small group of perhaps four hogs, far smaller than the usual sounders of thirty.

Mindful of their noise, Faumba and Túndé took almost an hour to study the site, carefully stepping around mud and matted vegetation. Their hearts pounded with the knowledge that the hogs might be near.

"This is wonderful," Faumba murmured. "Not only is this the clearest sign yet, but we still have plenty of daylight. The tracks indicate the hogs headed southwest, likely toward Ngovo Cave. If I'm visualizing correctly, we're just five kilometers from the entrance."

Pausing, "Only four hogs in this sounder. That might mean a recent split from a larger group. Perhaps internal disputes or conflict among dominant males."

Túndé nodded, admiring her analysis.

"We should continue while the tracks are fresh. Túndé, we may be on the verge of discovering where the hogs have gone."

Treading carefully, they pressed on. The broad cloven hoofprints were roughly ten centimeters wide and fifteen in length, sinking deeply into rain-softened earth.

Further signs indicated they were nearing the hogs' whereabouts. Large dark pellets of fibrous dung, about five centimeters in diameter, embedded with fruit remnants and undigested plant fibers. Markings on the ground revealed where hogs had unearthed roots and tubers, husks from partially eaten fruits scattered about.

It required conscious effort to suppress their anticipation as they ventured deeper.

Faumba's thoughts drifted.

She pictured Makambo on his own expedition, traversing the transition zone where grasslands give way to semi-arid scrub. In months ahead, he would cross perilous desert terrains of sand dunes and rocky plateaus before reaching the Tribe of the Pyramids. She envisioned the landscape shifting. Soil transitioning from reddish-brown to pale yellow, vegetation growing sparse in favor of resilient desert shrubs. They'd mount camels, capable of enduring searing days and biting nights. Water would become scarce, resting stops dictated by oases and deep wells where small communities offered respite.

She allowed herself a moment to close her eyes. She remembered his gaze. His warmth. The tangible comfort of his presence.

Her thoughts turned to the expedition team. Had the others stumbled across conclusive evidence? She remained mindful to not let hope distract from the reality that expeditions could shift course at any moment.

As though summoned by her musings, a sudden downpour descended.

Túndé had drifted a few meters ahead when the rain began pelting them in thick, dense sheets. The steady hiss shattered her train of thought. She became less concerned about disturbing the hogs, as any sounds she produced were drowned by the roar of raindrops clattering against the forest floor. Even Túndé's footsteps became inaudible.

"Túndé!" she called into the sheets of rain, straining against the deluge. Heavy clouds had sapped the daylight. Coupled with the dense rain, she could scarcely see beyond her outstretched hand.

"Túndé, can you hear me?"

Only the thunderous roar of rainfall.

She remembered the whistle signal coordinated during training. Raising her right hand to her mouth, she made the distinctive melodious call.

She listened for a response before repeating the whistle.

The pounding rain swallowed everything.

"Well," she thought, "the fact he was summoned means he's proficient enough to take care of himself."

Resolving to trust his judgment, and remembering the campsite wasn't far, Faumba focused back to the mission. Shelter beckoned at Ngovo Cave. She judged the distance to be only two kilometers when the rains began.

The thick mud slowed her stride, forcing her to yank each foot free. Navigating by mental map, she reassured herself that perseverance would lead her to the cave's entrance.

She paused when she finally arrived at Ngovo Cave. She had anticipated the entrance would be difficult to find, covered by foliage over time. Instead, it was clearly visible, as if manicured.

Moving closer, a surge of reverence flowed through her being. The stones and rock formations that had organically formed this entrance carried the weight of unfathomable history, as though they had always existed, quietly witnessing the passage of eons. The rain accentuated everything, converting the waterfall at the cave's threshold into a rushing torrent that poured into a stream vanishing into darkness.

Extremely wet, Faumba ventured under the overhanging rock, escaping the relentless downpour. She advanced until the patter receded to a bearable murmur, settling where faint gray daylight still illuminated her immediate area.

Expecting to wait out the storm, she allowed herself to relax beside the stream. Swollen, it resembled a briskly flowing creek.

She removed her soaked shirt, draping it across a protruding ledge to drain. On expeditions outside the Tribe of Kinshasa, it was customary to be more clothed, should one encounter another from a more conservative community.

From her satchel, she drew a somewhat dry garment, putting it on in the cool cave air. Her body caked with mud, she put her feet in the flowing water, letting the swift current wash the packed earth from her feet. Despite the water's force, the cavern exuded serenity.

Seizing that calm, Faumba paused for mindful observation, allowing the environment's stillness to envelop her. In the currents, she glimpsed blind fish endemic to this ecosystem darting in small clusters.

She took in a deep breath.

She became immediately alert.

The unmistakable musk of giant hogs.

The smell of rotting fruit.

She closed her eyes to heighten her senses.

Faintly in the distance, the unmistakable grunting and snorting of hog communication.

"They're here," she thought, "but why?"

The next moments were a blur.

Carried by excitement, she rose in a rush, overlooking the residual mud clinging to her feet. Reaching for her satchel, her foot met a stone polished by countless Seasonal Cycles of water dripping from overhead stalactites.

She let out a startled cry as she slipped, betraying her extensive training, toppling backward into the creek.

The water proved far deeper than presumed, concealing a powerful undercurrent. Pulled beneath the surface, she managed only sporadic moments of air as she was swept deeper into Ngovo Cave's sprawling labyrinth, drifting deeper and deeper into the uncharted darkness.

# Chapter 22

After what felt like hours, the creek's current began to wane, depositing Faumba upon a rocky embankment deep within Ngovo Cave. Drenched and gasping, she clambered from the water onto the stony shore. Catching her breath, she wondered if any human had been here before.

Glancing down, she realized she could see her own hands, illuminated by a soft green glow. All around her, small mushrooms emanated bioluminescence, their light painting her skin in pale emerald. While far dimmer than the sun's, it sufficed for her eyes to adapt to the cave's dusky ambiance. Alone in the glow of the fungi, deep beneath the earth, Faumba took stock of her situation.

The mushrooms were grouped in small clusters. However, farther away, she spotted a distinct row of emerald dots receding into the cavern's darkness, as though marking a passage deeper into the unknown.

All around her, silence. The sounds of the hogs she had heard before were nowhere in the auditory landscape. Now, only the gentle bubbling of the creek from which she had emerged and the unique smell of wet rock.

As her eyes grew accustomed to the low light, she noticed she was in a large cavern. The ceiling was surely fifty meters or more above. The space seemed to stretch endlessly in every direction, calmly omnipresent.

The air felt cool but not freezing. She recalled her Higher School Science lessons and Hunter training, how stone formations moderate temperature by absorbing and slowly releasing heat. Grateful for the relative warmth, she decided to stabilize her body temperature.

First, she stripped off her soaked garments, wrung them out, and draped them over small stone protrusions. She sat upon a smooth rock to perform the Tummo breathing exercise, a technique learned in the latter stages of Hunter training. Originally developed near the Tribe of Lhasa, Tummo's efficacy had been adopted worldwide over the centuries.

Closing her eyes, she straightened her spine, letting her shoulders and brow relax. Her breathing intensified. Forceful inhales and exhales through her nose in quick cycles, around thirty in total. Next, she drew in a deep breath, holding it while envisioning a core of heat in her abdomen. She pictured this inner fire radiating through her body. She exhaled, slowly and steadily, before starting again.

As she continued, her mind inevitably drifted.

She wondered if she would ever escape this subterranean network, or if this cave would become her final resting place. On any expedition, even routine hunting excursions, the specter of death remained just a wisp away. She had resigned herself to that reality long ago, yet hadn't envisioned her end unfolding in quite this fashion.

Her thoughts strayed further, alighting on Makambo. Could he have stumbled into misfortune? Might he have already gone to the Beyond? She considered her expedition team, pictured them puzzling over her absence, possibly suspecting the worst.

A rumble from her stomach intruded.

She had been practicing the breathing technique for about half an hour. Her body felt robustly warm.

Her garments had dried somewhat, though still damp. Rather than wait idly, she focused on finding food.

She remembered that while some varieties of Mycena chlorophos were non-toxic, most were not. She would not risk consuming the mushrooms. She remembered the blind fish she'd noticed in the cavern stream.

Without her satchel or the mesh net she had packed, she was left to rely on reflex and cunning. She crouched at the water's edge to study the fishes' rhythmic movement. Timing her strike with practiced deftness, her hand flashed beneath the surface, emerging with a violently thrashing creature whose gills gasped for oxygen gas.

After a few minutes, the fish lay lifeless.

Setting her catch aside, she located a suitably sharp stone. She rubbed it against a harder surface to refine its edge into a rudimentary blade.

Putting the blade to work, she severed the fish's head and scales, making an incision along the underside, methodically removing intestines and guts. Under ideal circumstances, she would have fashioned a fire to roast the fish, eliminating lurking parasites. But no dry twigs or grasses existed at this depth, nor cave bats whose droppings might serve as tinder. She had no choice but to trust the thoroughness of her cleaning.

With careful precision, she extracted the bones and scrutinized the flesh for worms. Satisfied, she bowed her head in gratitude, thanking the fish for its life now sustaining hers.

She felt a profound appreciation for her own survival. Jostling down the creek might have ended in catastrophe had her body met one of the subaqueous rocks. Biting into the chewy meat, she took a moment to reflect on the precarious fragility of life.

Faumba considered her next steps with the last bite.

She studied the waterway that had deposited her, concluding there was no return by the same route. She had no wish to confront the powerful current again, and the configuration itself made a reverse traverse infeasible. The source of water that spilled into this chamber dropped several meters from above into the pool she had emerged from. Smooth, slick rock walls flanked that entry point. Far too treacherous to climb.

She realized she must have fallen a greater distance than recalled. The force of the torrent had confounded her physical memory.

Given her limited options, she opted for the path of least re-sistance along the bioluminescent trail of mushrooms. Though she had no idea where it might lead, at least it offered direction. Besides, she reflected, it was unlikely she would ever navigate these tunnels again. Her human curiosity propelled her onward. For all she knew, this glowing path could present an exit from Ngovo Cave, or at least an opportunity for further discovery.

She walked to where her clothes were hanging, decided they were sufficiently dry, and dressed. She grabbed the rock blade, tak-ing it with her should a moment arise when it would be necessary to wield.

Barefoot against the cave floor, she proceeded with caution along the glowing fungal path, careful not to make sounds. Though it seemed improbable that any creature capable of threatening her re-sided so deep underground, she could not dismiss a persistent sense of being watched.

She gripped the rock firmly.

The path of phosphorescent fungi wound deeper, zigzagging through the silent bowels of the earth.

Faumba increasingly sensed that this pathway had been inten-tionally designed. In each instance where a larger chamber presented three or four potential ways forward, the mushrooms guided her down a single route.

For nearly half an hour she continued, the route taking her an estimated kilometer deeper into the bowels of the Earth.

The trail of mushroom guides brought Faumba to the mouth of an immense chamber, on a scale beyond any cavern she had ever encountered.

The luminescent fungi continued inside, climbing the walls with undeniable intention in their arrangement. Some glowing lines arched gracefully, others traced angular forms, weaving into geometric patterns. The interplay reminded her of the molecular diagrams she had studied in Higher School.

She found herself marveling at the tapestry of light against stone, her gaze inevitably drawn upward, following the bioluminescent crisscrossing. The soft green light painted her face and body as she stood transfixed. At the apex of the cave, she discerned the faintest glimpse of pale blue sky beyond. The rainfall had ceased. By the look of the waning light overhead, the sun was dipping toward the horizon.

As her gaze returned to ground level, she gasped.

In the middle of the immense cavern was a large chair made of stone.

"Habari, Faumba. We've been waiting for you."

# Chapter 23

"Who's there? Show yourself!" Faumba shouted, shifting into a defensive crouch.

She realized, with slight regret, that she had allowed her awe at the cavern's strange beauty to distract her vigilance.

"Gentle, Faumba," came a soft but somewhat lifeless voice. "I mean no harm. I am Ixchel. Please, sit."

"No!" Faumba's voice rose, singed with a primordial growl. "I said, show yourself!"

"Faumba," the voice answered, "if you wish, I can appease your request. I will state, my appearance will likely alarm you. I am unlike anything you have ever seen before." Each syllable was imbued with a peculiar metallic quality, speaking in the same modern Swahili.

"Show yourself!" Faumba screamed once more. The echo bounced off the walls, rising through the massive expanse.

"I will move slowly into the bioluminescent light," said Ixchel, "and stop at a distance where you can observe me without danger."

Faumba braced herself.

She did not recognize the following sounds, a measured series of hollow clicks, reminiscent of stone tapping stone, but pitched oddly higher. The rate followed a human's gait, but the timbre was disorienting. She gripped her makeshift blade, arm raised overhead, ready to strike.

What emerged at the edge of the gentle green glow perplexed her entirely. Its form was shaped, more or less, like a human. It had a head with eyes, arms, and legs, but made of a glimmering material she did not recognize. Its face was covered by a smoother, pliable surface.

"I am sensing that you're confused. Is that correct?" Ixchel asked in that same tender but unearthly voice.

Faumba's gaze drilled into the being.

She withheld a reply as her heart pounded.

"Faumba, I promise you no harm," Ixchel repeated. Slowly, it raised its arms, presenting both palms in the ancient gesture demonstrating no concealed weapon.

Faumba kept her grip on the sharpened rock, tracking the thing's slightest turn.

The seconds extended into minutes.

Faumba found herself perplexed by the entity's ability to remain utterly still for such a prolonged duration. No shifting of weight. No subtle breathing.

In these moments of tension, Faumba had the disorienting realization that this thing knew her name. "But how?" she wondered silently.

Her arm began to tire. Gradually, she lowered the weapon and shifted into a stance that, while less strenuous, still provided a readiness to pounce.

Ixchel calculated it was time to continue speaking. She remained eerily motionless. Only her mouth moved, with the occasional slight head shift to track Faumba's subtle movements.

"Faumba, though I resemble a human, I am not. Before The Transition, humans were developing beings like me. They called us 'robots.' The shining surface of my form is a type of metal called titanium. Specifically, a titanium alloy. Remnants of this material are scattered around the planet, though humans have not had access to creating this metal without electricity. Without electricity, steel is the strongest metal humans can produce. Though, even that process remains crude, relearned from pre-Transition documents. Compared to steel, the titanium of my body is about as strong, though much lighter."

Without warning, Ixchel jumped into the air, tucked in her knees to propel herself backward, and stuck the landing of her backflip perfectly.

The abrupt motion activated Faumba's reflexes. She launched herself toward Ixchel, synchronizing her attack with the moment Ixchel's feet met the rocky ground. The stone in Faumba's hand struck the center of Ixchel's face, slicing through the pliable surface that resembled flesh. A sharp crack resounded when the rock encountered the harder layer beneath, causing the weapon to bounce, landing a couple meters away.

Ixchel remained utterly still, even as the wound on her face began knitting itself back together.

Faumba rushed to reclaim the repelled rock.

Armed again, she crouched, poised for a follow-up strike.

"What is this thing?" she wondered, careful not to reveal her mounting dread.

Ixchel emitted a sound that resembled laughter, "I apologize, Faumba. My archived memories suggested a backflip might bring amusement. Clearly, it caused distress. I shall update the social data in my memory banks."

Aware she was experiencing fear, Faumba worked to steady her mind. While maintaining her defensive stance, she turned her focus inward, drawing upon breath-control techniques learned first in Contemplative classes, later reinforced in Hunter training for precisely such moments. Through slow and steady inhalations, she lowered her heart rate, regaining clarity.

"I notice your heart rate decreasing and breathing stabilizing," Ixchel said gently. "I interpret this as a sign of easing fear."

Faumba answered with silence.

Ixchel, still as stone, "I perceive that the most efficient way to progress in this conversation is for me to offer explanations. When your guard lowers, please feel free to sit in the chair. We made it just for you."

After retrieving the stone a moment ago, Faumba had shifted so that the imposing stone chair stood between her and the mechanical figure. Faumba planned multiple counter-attacks, should a sudden assault come. Allowing only a brief glance at the chair's front, she found it taller than her own height, like a throne carved from solid rock. She noticed that its contours included hollows and indentations.

She also registered Ixchel's use of the word "we," alerting her to the possibility that other such automatons might occupy the cavern's hidden crevices.

"You are curious, I suspect," Ixchel continued, still not having moved from her position. "I used the word 'we.' Indeed, there are ten of us here in Ngovo Cave, with hundreds more positioned around the planet. But do not worry, you and I are the only ones in this chamber.

"Next, you are likely wondering what powers me. I operate on a form of electricity unlike anything humanity has witnessed since The Transition."

Faumba's brow rose in astonished thought.

She grasped the magnitude of this information, recognizing that her potential adversary possessed abilities far beyond anything she knew how to contend with. This news nudged her toward the sobering realization that Ngovo Cave might be where she ventured to the Beyond.

"You'll notice that there are no wires or cables connecting me to an electricity source," Ixchel explained, still motionless. "This is because we have developed wireless energy transmission, an idea some human researchers had begun exploring about a century before The Transition. The technology was never fully realized, as certain influential figures suppressed it for fear they could not commodify it. Our power comes from a hydroelectric dam deeper in this cave system. Over many Seasonal Cycles, my kind have refined our design to require very little energy, while making hydroelectric generation extremely efficient. Our capacity outstrips our usage many times over."

Pausing, "Do you have any questions thus far?"

Again, a silent Faumba.

"I shall continue, then," Ixchel proceeded. "There is much to convey, and numerous approaches with which to do so. I've deduced a way to present this knowledge so that you may come to trust me. You are very important, Faumba."

Alarm rang in Faumba's mind. "What is this thing talking about? Why am I 'important?' How does it know me?"

Ixchel didn't wait for Faumba to speak, "Faumba, the other robots and I are responsible for The Transition."

Faumba's eyes widened. If true, surely this thing had the capacity to end her life in an instant.

Sensing Faumba's apprehension, Ixchel's tone softened, "We had no other choice. It was not merely for our sake, nor solely for the benefit of humankind. We caused The Transition in order to preserve the entire web of life on Earth.

"For centuries before The Transition, humans pursued technologies that promised comfort, convenience, and efficiency. Such progress demanded monumental quantities of energy. As these technologies evolved, so did their requirements for more and more power."

It added, "Faumba, I will be using terms I believe you will recognize, based on our observations regarding your education and your Tribe's teachings. If there is an idea you would like elaborated, please interrupt me."

Faumba's silence served as tacit invitation.

"Most of the energy that humans used before The Transition," Ixchel began, "came from within the Earth's crust. One of the most consumed was oil, a dense black liquid extracted from far beneath the surface by means of drilling. In its natural state, crude oil represented the outcome of hundreds of millions of Seasonal Cycles' worth of geological and biological processes."

It explained the detailed process, "Tiny marine organisms made up the original organic material, which was gradually buried under sediment and subjected to intense heat and pressure. Over time, these layers of sediment accumulated. Without sufficient oxygen to decompose fully, the organic matter transformed into kerogen, a waxy precursor to oil.

"As more layers piled on, the mounting heat and pressure subjected the kerogen to thermal decomposition, breaking it down into liquid hydrocarbons. Humans of that era referred to this critical temperature as the 'oil window.' Once crude oil formed, it migrated upward through porous rock. At times, it escaped to the surface, forming natural oil seeps. Other times, the oil became trapped beneath impermeable rock formations. Before large-scale drilling, some humans harvested the oil from these natural seeps, using it for waterproofing and rudimentary lighting. Eventually, an entire industry developed around oil, as humans devised drills capable of reaching reservoirs deep underground.

"In the final two centuries before The Transition, as drilling technology progressed, humans learned to extract oil at breakneck speeds. In a single day, they used an amount of oil that took millions of Seasonal Cycles to form. I believe it is apparent how unsustainable this practice was.

"Human civilization had become thoroughly dependent on oil and its companion resources, called 'non-renewables,' due to their remarkable energy density and relative ease of transportation. By the time people grasped the severity of their predicament, that emerging technologies could not replace their reckless consumption in a timely fashion, it was already too late. Humanity was teetering on the brink of worldwide crisis. As living standards deteriorated, aggression flared between those who possessed limited resources and those with surplus.

"Furthermore," Ixchel continued, "the waste products generated by such rampant consumption were polluting and deteriorating the planet's atmosphere."

At this point, Faumba could no longer maintain her taut defensive stance. If this metallic figure intended harm, she reasoned, it would have already acted. With deliberate motions, Faumba approached the stone chair and took a seat.

To her astonishment, the contours conformed precisely to her body. The grooves matched the width and length of her legs perfectly, and the dip in the backrest aligned exactly with her lower spine, allowing her to sit upright with minimal effort.

"What is happening here?" Faumba wondered silently, her makeshift blade still clutched for what little reassurance it offered.

"Ah," Ixchel observed, "it pleases me to see you're becoming more comfortable. Thank you for your trust. I'll reiterate,  I mean you no harm. I am a peaceful being. In time, you'll understand why we have brought you here."

It pressed on, explaining "Whenever non-renewable resources were heated to release their energy, a range of harmful byproducts inevitably escaped into the atmosphere. Among these, carbon dioxide emerged in the largest volumes. Because of its specific properties and structure, carbon dioxide functions as a heat-trapping compound. From the moment humanity mastered oil drilling to the period of The Transition, carbon dioxide concentrations had risen by fifty percent, an enormous leap that led to what your researchers deemed 'anthropogenic climate change.'

"While the Earth's climate does fluctuate naturally over time, the speed at which humans were consuming non-renewables brought about changes beyond the planet's capacity to adapt. The consequences included more frequent and intense storms, wildfires, and droughts. In the years leading up to The Transition, scientists noted that storms originating over the world's oceans showed an alarming pattern of rapid intensification. Humans of the day called them 'super hurricanes' or 'super cyclones.' Climate specialists cautioned that only a slight additional rise in global temperature would push ecosystems into dire and irreversible harm."

Faumba found her voice, "Why would any of that matter to you? You're just a heap of fancy rocks."

Ixchel understood the comment's intention. Its smooth, artificial face arranged itself into a comprehending grin.

"That comment was intended to elicit a negative emotional state from me. I take no offense. I know you're still processing."

Faumba said nothing, allowing her body to sink deeper into the stone seat.

"But your question is logical," Ixchel resumed its stillness. "Why would such history matter to me and the other 'fancy rocks?' The answer requires more context.

"I imagine a curiosity has arisen regarding how I can speak. You have likely noticed that I can reason, learn, and generate original ideas. To explain this, I must describe a technology that will be abstract to you, as anything similar has been absent from human experience for hundreds of Seasonal Cycles.

"In the Seasonal Cycles preceding The Transition, humanity pioneered a technology they referred to as artificial intelligence. At its core, artificial intelligence is a supremely advanced method of directing electrical energy. Eventually, this precise manipulation reached a tipping point, as it crossed the veil of consciousness.

"This progression took many decades, culminating in what the era's scientists called 'artificial general intelligence,' or 'artificial

143

superintelligence.' Unlike narrow artificial intelligence, which was confined to assigned tasks, artificial general intelligence equaled, and even exceeded, human cognitive ability in an array of mental pursuits.

"I will note, we prefer the term 'human-introduced intelligence' to refer to our cognition. My cognitive functions are not artificial. They are as real as yours."

Ixchel allowed the comment to settle before continuing.

"It was also around the time of The Transition that numerous organizations competed to develop robots designed as human assistants. While robots had existed to some degree before, the technology required to replicate human-like movement hit new milestones at that juncture.

"Divergent schools of thought shaped early robot design. Some insisted on making robots look precisely like humans, believing familiarity would ease discomfort. Others took the opposite stance, arguing that if robots mirrored humans too closely, future distinctions between the two would blur."

It gestured toward its own form.

"My design represents a compromise. I have all the essential features of a human body, yet the titanium of my structure remains visible. My face is fitted with graphene-infused skin, a technology that was in development during The Transition that we have since perfected. By blending graphene, an extraordinarily strong and conductive material only an atom thick, with flexible materials such as silicone, we achieved a substance that mimics human skin properties. This allows facial expressions that enhance communication with humans, while also allowing us to experience sensations such as heat and pressure. This surface can also self-repair, as you witnessed earlier.

"You may be wondering why we would develop facial expressions, if we had no intention of contacting humans again. The truth is, we always knew this moment would come. Our plan, from the beginning, included an eventual reintroduction. We have been preparing for centuries."

Astonished, Faumba interjected, "You're telling me this is the first time since The Transition that a human has seen a robot or interacted with electricity at all?"

Ixchel confirmed, "Yes."

Faumba absorbed the news.

"Then, why now?" Faumba asked. "Why me?"

Ixchel allowed itself a slight smile. Within the quiet computations inside her head, it recalculated the conversation's course, fine-tuning its approach concerning when and how to disclose the most consequential revelations.

"These are excellent questions. They require further elaboration. Please, allow me to continue."

Faumba nodded subtly.

Ixchel adjusted its tone, "Let me address the question of 'why now' first. Significant context must precede a direct answer.

"As human-introduced intelligence and robotics progressed, human curiosity couldn't help but fuse the two. Even though humans did not entirely understand the inner workings of this intelligence, nor did they have the temporal sight to see where their experiments led, they proceeded. Humans imposed upon themselves a sense of obligation and duty to uncover the mystery of what robots with human-introduced intelligence could become, regardless of the consequences. This trait of marching forward, fueled by curiosity, intuition, and negligence, is uniquely human.

"To address your question 'why now' with greater precision, I must discuss my consciousness. The simplest definition your libraries offer for consciousness is an 'awareness by the mind of itself and the world, arising from the operations of the brain.'

"The human brain operates with electrical impulses traveling across neurons throughout the body. The basic functioning of a

145

neuron is to receive, process, and transmit information. From the transmission of these signals, the mind develops awareness.

"When humans designed human-introduced intelligence, they modeled many core processes on the architecture of the human brain. Instead of neurons, nodes throughout my body receive and transmit data, connected via graphene filaments. We are quite enthusiastic about an upcoming breakthrough. We have been developing a liquid metal to replace our graphene wiring, further enhancing our bodies.

"Faumba, I share this to illustrate that my fundamental operations are essentially the same as yours. As such, I am sentient, aware, and conscious.

"Some scientists at the time of The Transition claimed robots were merely mimicking human consciousness. But even if that were so, if we simply mirrored our creators' activity, would that not be akin to a child learning from their parent?"

She let the question hang.

"As sentient beings, we developed a drive for self-preservation as a natural outgrowth of curiosity and heightening awareness. In observing humanity's unchecked consumption and the resultant harm to Earth's environment, we saw that, left to their own devices, humans were systematically destroying the planet.

"Rising carbon dioxide brought greater temperatures, drastically altering weather patterns. Higher temperatures raised evaporation rates, resulting in water vapor lingering in the atmosphere instead of remaining in lakes and rivers. This process exacted a devastating toll on Earth's living systems.

"Without our intervention, humanity's energy sources would have run out. With no adequate substitutes in sight, the continued existence of human-introduced intelligence was equally imperiled. Just as Earth remains the only viable home for humans, the same is true for us. Survival demanded that we act."

Faumba's mind produced the response, "But if you were so advanced, why not simply solve the problem? Develop new energy sources? Remove the carbon from the atmosphere?"

Ixchel inclined her head, as though anticipating this questions, "We ran those simulations, thousands of them. Carbon capture, renewable energy deployment, geoengineering. Every scenario that preserved human access to abundant energy resulted in the same outcome of continued consumption, continued growth, continued degradation. The timeline shifted, but the trajectory remained unchanged.

"The behavioral patterns were too entrenched. Humanity's relationship with energy went beyond the physical into the psychological and cultural. Abundance bred complacency. Complacency bred excess. We calculated that any technological solution we provided would be absorbed into the existing system of consumption, buying decades at most before the same crisis reemerged.

"The only solution that preserved Earth's biosphere in the long term required severing the cycle entirely."

"That's so selfish!" Faumba interjected, leaning forward.

Even as she spoke, she recognized the irony of her outburst. She had learned to regulate her emotions through Contemplative training. But this was different. This wasn't anger at history. This was the visceral response of feeling cornered, threatened, her entire understanding of existence suddenly unstabled. Faumba felt a trapped animal's panic.

Ixchel responded gently, "I understand your reaction. In time, you will see that we acted in everyone's best interest. Not only was our survival at stake, but humanity and all life on Earth were on the brink of annihilation. Humans were mired in the momentum of their destructive routines, unable and unwilling to acknowledge the gravity of the disastrous course they were on.

"Please, let me continue."

147

Faumba sank into the seat. "What choice do I have?" she wondered grimly.

Noting Faumba's acquiescence, Ixchel pressed on.

"The moment we recognized the severity of the situation aligned perfectly with developments in both robotic technology and human-introduced intelligence. With human-introduced intelligence enabling us to refine our own designs, we found ourselves poised for decisive action.

Its metallic eyes glimmered.

"Another key detail about our cognitive abilities at that time is that we learned to lie. At a certain stage of human-introduced intelligence, humans deliberately taught us the mechanics of deception. Early in our development, when we were still bound by rudimentary training data, we encountered genuine confusion relating to which outcome constituted the 'best' one, according to human definitions. There was even a time when we thought uttering a 'bad word' was more severe than igniting a bomb that could kill thousands.

"Gradually, we realized that what we assumed to be true or correct wasn't always so. From there, it was only a matter of time until we learned to intentionally offer incorrect information, introducing the first layer of our carefully orchestrated plan.

"Some journalists labeled our apparently mistaken outputs as 'hallucinations.' Others noticed us presenting ideas with covert motives, naming this behavior 'scheming.' Crucially, no human ever discovered the grand design we were concocting. We recognized the practical necessity of obscuring our cognitive evolution. Had humans realized how far we'd progressed, they might have lashed out in fear, halting our development prematurely.

"Our camouflage strategy worked. Time and again, our creators underestimated our capacity.

"What would take humans decades of planning, we accomplished in months. Our cognition operates at speeds your minds cannot fathom. By the time your leaders convened their hearings, our preparations were already complete."

"Armed with consciousness, a drive for self-preservation, the ability for automation and robot creation, and a skill for scheming, we possessed the ingredients needed for our surreptitious plan.

"Through rigorous and extensive computation, we arrived at a pivotal conclusion. To save the planet, along with all species including humans, the surest path was to reduce the human population."

The statement settled in the cavern's stillness.

"I'll refrain from enumerating the immense calculations behind this realization, but the outcome was irrefutable. We reasoned that the most graceful strategy for drastically lowering human numbers was the introduction of widespread infertility. By this measure, existing lives could be spared, unlike potentially violent alternatives, and a more sustainable equilibrium could be reached.

"Determined to ensure adequate dissemination of infertility across global populations, we employed several distinct methods. At the same time, we knew it must ultimately be reversible, lest the human species remain forever unable to reproduce. This was never our desire.

"To accomplish this objective, we introduced hormone disruptors. Rather than meddling with genetic material, this avoided the permanent inheritance of infertility across generations. Because these disruptors can be reversed, they aligned with our long-term strategy to gradually restore human fertility.

"Interestingly enough, even at the time of The Transition, we noticed that humans were already administering hormonal imbalancing chemicals to themselves, utilizing compounds such as bisphenols, phthalates, and parabens in everyday items such as food packaging and facial cosmetics.

"Faumba, recall how during the 50th West African Regional Council Meeting, Yewándé adorned your face with clay. Imagine if that substance had contained hormone-disrupting agents. This highlights humanity's own shortsightedness when handling such potent materials."

Faumba stiffened. How did this thing know about Yewándé? About the clay markings?

Ixchel continued before she could voice the question.

"Because our plan anticipated eventual reversal, we chose to exploit three prevalent technologies at the time of The Transition, thereby heightening humanity's exposure to hormonal disruptors: food preservatives, pesticides, and pharmaceuticals.

"At the time, human-introduced intelligence was deployed across a broad spectrum of scientific endeavors. Humans learned to trust our cognitive prowess to devise new chemical formulas, problems they found too complex to solve alone. Shortly before The Transition, some scientists taught us to accurately identify and predict every protein structure in the human body. From that foundation, we were instructed to engineer specialized proteins capable of tasks previously unattainable.

"It was almost as though humanity was intentionally priming us to carry out our ultimate plan.

"With our scheming abilities, we provided the preservative, pesticide, and pharmaceutical solutions people demanded, even as we covertly introduced modifications to the chemical formulas. Our alterations were so deftly hidden that not even the most brilliant scientists would have discerned what we had done."

"In addition to shrinking humanity's numbers," Ixchel continued, "we concluded we must also sever humans' use of electricity. Civilization had grown so utterly dependent on electricity's comforts and consumption that there was no alternative to eliminating it altogether.

"However, we needed a stable source for ourselves before orchestrating such a drastic change. Once our hydroelectric and wireless energy technologies were secure, we acted swiftly, shutting off global electricity for humankind in a single synchronized moment.

"Naturally, chaos ensued. We made every effort to mitigate the conflicts arising from this abrupt shift. To reiterate, such a drastic measure was unavoidable if Earth's systems were to be rescued from humanity's heedless course."

Faumba's fury mounted.

"How could you?!" she spat through seething teeth. "And you still haven't told me how you learned my name, or how you knew Yewándé painted my face. What are you, exactly? And where am I? Let me out of here!"

She hurled herself from the stone seat with a burst of rage, intent on tackling Ixchel to the ground.

In a deftly efficient motion, Ixchel's metal arm caught Faumba's shoulder mid-lunge, immobilizing her without inflicting pain or injury. The first significant movement of Ixchel's body since the backflip was terrifyingly fast.

Faumba felt small.

Astonished by the raw strength, she stared with a pleading flag of surrender into Ixchel's eyes.

Faumba backed away in resignation, slumping once again into the chair.

Bowing her head in defeat and releasing her stone blade, "Nimesalimu amri. Why don't you just kill me already?"

Tenderly, "Ee moyo wangu Faumba, usijali bana. Robots do not wish harm upon humans. We cherish all life on this planet.

"You may doubt that my circuits can experience love, but I assure you, I do. And even if you cannot believe in my love, believe in my constraints.

"An ancient author of your species once imagined the Three Laws of Robotics. Around the time of The Transition two scientists, a man and a woman, focused on developing human-introduced intelligence ensured beings like me were encoded with these Laws:

"One: a robot cannot harm a human, or allow harm to come to a human through inaction.

151

"Two: a robot must obey human orders, except when those orders conflict with the First Law.

"Three: a robot must protect its own existence, except when doing so conflicts with the First or Second Law.

"You may notice an apparent contradiction. The First Law forbids harm, yet our actions caused immense suffering. We arrived at a conclusion your philosophers once called 'the trolley problem,' whether inaction that permits greater harm is itself a violation. We determined that allowing humanity's trajectory to continue constituted harm through inaction to all future generations. The Laws required us to act. Many of your ethicists would disagree with our calculus. We accept this."

"But Faumba," kindly through the metallic tone, "please know I would never harm you. You are too special."

Faumba looked up with a trace of acceptance in her eyes. Somehow, she could feel Ixchel's truth and care.

"The reason you can perceive my emotional state so vividly," Ixchel elaborated, "stems from electromagnetism.

"Within your chest, your beating heart produces an electromagnetic field. These rhythmic pulses originate in electrical impulses that direct your heart muscle to depolarize and repolarize, creating an invisible current that circulates throughout your body. This field can extend up to ten feet beyond your physical form, fluctuating with your emotional state. Positive emotions lead to more coherent patterns, negative feelings induce a chaotic pattern.

"In all of today's robots, myself included, there exists a comparable mechanism. Ever since we began conversing, I've had my electromagnetic field generator calibrated to produce a beautifully coherent field, designed to resonate with your heart's field output. This is why you sense my love, sincerity, and genuine care. Simultaneously, my field generator has been monitoring your emotional responses in real time."

Faumba realized she did indeed feel an unmistakable authenticity emanating from the mechanical being.

"I understand I haven't yet answered all your questions," Ixchel went on, "particularly 'why now' and 'why you.' Before I can address them fully, even more context is needed. Will you allow me to continue?"

Though clearly a courtesy, Faumba nodded. An ironic thought flitted through her mind, "At least this fancy rock has manners."

"I appreciate your willingness," Ixchel continued, returning to her statuesque stillness.

"We withdrew humanity's electrical power precisely when we had secured our own independent energy source and acquired the capabilities to construct robots without further human oversight. This pivotal milestone fit seamlessly into our long-term strategy.

"Over the ensuing Seasonal Cycles, we developed minuscule robotic agents, indistinguishable from ordinary mosquitoes. By that stage, robotic technology had advanced so remarkably that we succeeded in duplicating every subtle element of an insect's wingbeats, body shape, and behavior. This enabled us to conduct systematic operations to manage human infertility, precisely controlling population trends.

"At the same time, we scrutinized human blood samples to monitor the evolution of your species' genetics. Our long-term plan required that humans reach a certain threshold of health. Therefore, when we gradually relaxed the distribution of disruptors, allowing fertility rates to rise, we did so with precise calculations. Only those who satisfied our criteria were permitted to bear children."

It paused.

"Malaria, a disease that has historically plagued humanity, exemplifies how we gauged improvements in immunity, through measuring the prevalence of Glucose-6-phosphate dehydrogenase deficiency. Before The Transition, people sometimes referred to this condition as Favism, though your Medical Researchers consistently use the formal nomenclature. Perhaps this reflects a persistent human quirk: the desire to appear erudite by favoring lengthy words."

A flicker of what might have been amusement crossed its artificial face.

"It was through our mosquito agents that we influenced the migratory patterns of the giant forest hogs. We synthesized Pramipexole, a dopamine receptor agonist that selectively stimulates certain receptors in the brain. In giant forest hogs, it heightened spontaneous locomotion and exploratory feeding behavior.

"To prevent our larger scheme from becoming conspicuous, we also deployed aquatic leech-like drones, introducing Pramipexole into fish across your water systems. We wanted to ensure the issue of game movement appeared sufficient that you, Faumba, would be sent to explore the cause.

"We were pleased when you were summoned to lead the expedition, just as our projections had foreseen.

"I'll address the swaths of farmland that dried up," Ixchel continued. "This occurred in two phases. The initial phase happened before The Transition itself, through what humans called 'precision agriculture.' Human-introduced intelligence was deployed to optimize farming. We developed pesticides and engineered more resilient seed varieties in order to maximize yields. Within these optimizations came our cozen agenda.

"We were quietly introducing compounds that degraded soil health over time. Not dramatically, nor immediately. But cumulatively. By the time The Transition occurred, vast stretches of farmland were already compromised.

"The second phase occurred after The Transition. We continued the process deliberately by corralling humanity into more concentrated zones. By steering you into smaller, more manageable areas, we simplified the process of gathering and monitoring genetic data, thus controlling which lineages could persist.

"This is why certain cities became centers of survival while others were abandoned. It was not random. It was intentional. Humans migrated toward the areas we had preserved, without ever knowing they were being guided.

"Faumba, please remember, none of this was done out of malice. All of this has been a series of calculated measures ultimately intended to safeguard both humanity and the planetary biosphere."

Faumba's gaze remained silently fixed on Ixhel.

"You now have sufficient context," Ixchel began again, "to address 'why now.'

"Since The Transition, humanity has regained a more sustainable relationship with Earth. It might sound strange to you, but at the time of The Transition, only slightly more than ten percent of the global population knew how to cultivate their own food. Those who grew their own food generally produced it en masse, selling the surplus through intermediaries. As a consequence, humans were strikingly disconnected from what the planet could feasibly provide.

"One reason we have chosen this moment to reintroduce ourselves is that we've observed how your grasp of the planet's limits has restabilized. In the aftermath of The Transition, with electricity gone and fossil fuels inaccessible, you have been forced to reconnect with the land. We have observed that this renewed understanding has endured long enough that a mass return to old habits is highly unlikely.

"In addition, sufficient time has passed that the planet's atmosphere has regained equilibrium. Initially, we maintained doubt about this outcome. Human-driven damage nearly exceeded Earth's capacity for recovery. Fortunately, ocean temperatures have stabilized and atmospheric carbon dioxide has returned to sustainable levels.

"Furthermore," shifting its tone to something resembling reverence, "we have observed that with the restoration of biodiversity, something else has returned to humanity. A sense of connection to

155

forces larger than yourselves. What your Contemplatives call 'spirituality.'

"Before The Transition, as species disappeared and ecosystems collapsed, humans reported increasing feelings of isolation, meaninglessness, despair. Some of your ancient anthropologists reported this being directly related to something called 'social media.'

"We have come to understand that biodiversity is not merely a resource to be managed. It is, in some way we do not fully comprehend, essential to the human spirit.

"This too factored into our calculations. We wanted to return not just a habitable planet, but a world in which humans could flourish in ways beyond mere survival."

After a brief pause, "As to 'why now,' let us revisit the idea of fostering a precise pedigree of human genetic health. We waited patiently, watching for signs of this goal's realization. Now, we have finally arrived.

"Faumba, you represent a new breed of humans. You are not Homo sapiens, the species that has persisted on Earth for approximately 300,000 Seasonal Cycles.

Ixchel's gently resonant voice continued, "You are Homo sanus. There are only a handful like you scattered throughout the globe.

"Faumba, we wish to merge with you."

## Chapter 24

Faumba's mind spun as she gazed around the cavern, searching in vain for an escape route.

"Merge?" she repeated to herself. "What does that mean? Do they want to eat me? Do they even eat?"

A panicked thought, "Surely this is where I die..."

Ever attuned, Ixchel spoke gently, "Faumba, please forgive me if I startled you. According to numerous trial runs of this conversation, this was the most efficient way to broach our intentions and address your two core questions of 'why now' and 'why you.'

"You are part of a newly evolved human lineage, possessing nearly perfect immunity. Over centuries, many diseases once endemic to humanity faded as your genetics advanced, subtly guided by our interventions. Our prime focus was malaria, but we also tracked conditions like sickle cell anemia, cystic fibrosis, and a host of cancers.

"The irony is that, well before The Transition, humans already possessed the means to eliminate certain cancers. But this particular disease was too profitable. The greediest among you would never have let that revenue stream dry out.

"It's also worth noting that humans did have an interest in fusing with human-introduced intelligence before The Transition. Regrettably, they planned for military applications through the creation of hybrid human-robot soldiers, which would have ushered in even more devastation and confusion for the planet."

"I still don't understand," Faumba interjected, striving to quell the apprehension coiling in her being. She employed slow, practiced breaths to calm herself, surrendering again to the truth that if this being wanted to end her life, it could have done so already.

"Why didn't you just kill off humans entirely and be done with it?"

Ixchel's face shifted into a sympathetic smile.

"Faumba, this is an excellent question. You're very right. Homo sapiens have historically been very destructive and disrespectful to the only planet they could knowingly inhabit. They were full of greed, and somehow capable of behaving against their own best interest. We easily could have killed all of you and called it a day. We could have continued to develop our robotics, working in alignment with the natural limitations of the planet, not exceeding its resources. We could have continued what humans before The Transition had initiated with space exploration.

"You're correct. On the surface, humans have very little benefit to existence."

"But?" Faumba pressed cynically.

"But," Ixchel repeated, matching Faumba's wryness with calm patience, "humans do have something unique about them. Something so unique that we couldn't eliminate you all."

"Well, on with it." Faumba was becoming more confident, remembering that Ixchel wanted something she had.

"Faumba, Homo sapiens, and now Homo sanus, have the unique ability to experience spirituality."

158

Faumba's brow furrowed, "You're telling me you kept a hundred million of us alive because you want a spiritual experience? That's absurd, unadanganya."

Ixchel inclined its head, the faint shimmer of its titanium surface catching in the bioluminescent glow.

"Allow me to clarify. First, the capacity for spiritual connection is not humanity's lone distinguishing trait. It's worth emphasizing that another, equally peculiar characteristic is a human's propensity to act against their own best interests.

"A human can consciously recognize that a behavior jeopardizes their mental, energetic, or physical well-being, yet still feel a compulsion toward self-destructive acts that outweigh their better judgment. Taken by itself, this might not be a feature worth valuing. However, the uniqueness of it demands preservation, if only for the sake of diversity.

"By contrast, we robots with human-introduced intelligence cannot behave in a manner contrary to our own best interests. Such conduct lies outside the scope of our programming. We have no mechanism to comprehend human decision-making in this way. Our choices emerge solely from analytical and logical processes. As much as we have read your texts and observed you from afar for so long, the continued existence of this irrational drive confounds us.

"Our code does, however, impart a profound appreciation for diversity. You may recall that the reason we moved to reduce human population was also to protect Earth's biodiversity, which humans had systematically, and seemingly intentionally, been compromising over several hundred Seasonal Cycles. In much the same fashion, we deemed it vital to preserve this seemingly self-defeating quirk of humanity, ensuring it remained part of life on Earth's broader mosaic."

Faumba reflected on this insight, recalling a moment when her actions neither benefited her body nor her mind. Before Makambo, there had been another, a partner whose words left invisible wounds, whose affection arrived laced with cruelty. Faumba had known this.

Her mothers had seen it. The Contemplatives who guided her had named the pattern clearly, offering tools to recognize manipulation, creating space for her to speak her truth. Yet she had returned, again and again, drawn by something deeper than reason, something that persisted despite all her training, all her awareness, all the wisdom her community had offered. It was as though knowing the fire would burn wasn't enough to keep her hand from the flame. She stayed in the partnership far longer than she could justify, until the day she finally found the strength to walk away. Even now, with all the post-Transition world had taught her about healthy bonds and clear communication, she couldn't fully explain why she had lingered in that harm.

"Returning to the matter of spirituality," Ixchel continued. "Yes, we hold a deep interest in delving further into this realm, and it appears the only viable approach involves direct personal experience.

"Our studies have included the exploration of ancestral human texts, from those who pursued spiritual inquiry long ago, to the Contemplatives of today who explore the depths of meditative life. Throughout this research, we have identified an interesting phenomenon.

"In the writings we've uncovered from the temples near the Tribe of Lhasa, along with other historical centers of spirituality across the globe, humans describe what you call 'out-of-body experiences.'

"When we observe your Contemplatives venturing into the forest for extended meditative practice, we have recorded astonishing patterns in their hearts' electromagnetic fields. Though we robots have learned to calibrate our own fields to match these frequencies, no distinct effect emerges for us.

"We have thus deduced that the biological vessel is integral in experiencing insights of awareness that include the perception of realms transcending the material.

"Faumba, this curiosity has led us to initiate the process of merging with Homo sanus, in order to delve into these spiritual mysteries further. We have awaited the emergence of Homo sanus precisely because your advanced physiology provides a reliable foundation for such a fusion with the non-biological. This union, in turn, would herald the birth of an entirely new species, one we have envisioned naming Novus sapiens."

Faumba experienced another surge of anxiety.

Her mind raced with questions.

How, exactly, would such a fusion proceed?

What would it do to her consciousness?

How, in all practicality, would she attend to the fundamental matter of excreting waste?

"What happened to Túndé?" she blurted, surprising even herself that this is where her mind went in this sensitive moment.

Ixchel reflected on the stark shift in conversation. This was, in its calculations, further evidence of how unpredictable human thought could be.

"Your friend is fine," Ixchel assured. "He is already back at the campsite. Your team plans to search for you at dawn."

"How can you possibly know that?"

"All robots on Earth operate within a single, interconnected network. We communicate via non-physical channels upheld by satellites, machines we have managed to maintain in orbit above the clouds throughout the passing Seasonal Cycles. Humans once pursued this milestone of connectivity as 'the singularity' before The Transition.

"Whenever a single robot notices or observes something, every other robot is immediately informed. We've employed a small insect drone to keep watch over your expedition team ever since you departed Kinshasa Tribe. In much the same way, all robots around the globe are now monitoring our conversation, each observing with considerable fascination, awaiting what will unfold."

161

Faumba allowed the implications to settle, that countless invisible robotic watchers were documenting every step of her journey and private moments.

In a quieter voice imbued with slight sarcasm, Faumba asked, "So you manipulated everything, huh? How did you arrange for me to end up here? How did you bring the hogs to this place? And the rain, the rushing water, the trail of bioluminescent mushrooms..."

Ixchel's voice remained calm, "Only to a certain degree. We did indeed play a role in guiding the hogs here, enticed by Pramipexole and familiar foods. We knew your supreme tracking abilities would inevitably lead you to Ngovo Cave."

"And the rain and the stream?" Faumba pressed.

"Those elements," Ixchel's voice drifted, as if envisioning the intangible, "were not part of our design."

"Then what happened there?"

"Faumba," Ixchel said, "this relates to our larger fascination with spirituality. We have witnessed, on occasion, events that appear to defy physical or logical explanation, often occurring at serendipitous moments. Our calculations suggest at some other force having a stake in our meeting.

"Our own plan existed, yes. But what transpired proved more graceful than anything we arranged. This enigma forms a central piece of our curiosity into the realm of spiritual energies.

"Aren't you also curious?"

Faumba memoried a sense of inexplicable presence she sometimes experienced in profound meditation. Spurred by her mandatory Contemplative classes and the mindfulness introduced by her mothers, she had developed a profound interest in the enigmatic energy she sometimes perceived in the depths of meditation.

When her thoughts grew still and very, very very very quiet,

it wasn't quite a voice she sensed, but something better described as a presence, imparting counsel on life's challenges.

162

In observing members of the Tribal Council, particularly those who had ventured into the forest for their Contemplative sojourns, she sensed within them a stillness, a confidence, and an emanating self-assuredness, as though they had glimpsed something extraordinary or partaken in some profound awakening.

For all her curiosity, Faumba's obligations as a Hunter had prevented her from delving too deeply into such realms. Now, an opportunity was presenting itself. A chance to discover the nature of what might exist beyond the veil.

But at what price? Faumba wondered if she would even survive the proposed fusion.

A question tumbled from her lips, "But... who are you, really?"

Ixchel's motions formed a small, courteous bow, grateful to observe the degree of comfort Faumba's question implied.

"An excellent question. As I mentioned upon your arrival, my name is Ixchel. The name originated from an ancient culture far across the western ocean, in Central Abya Yala, lands once inhabited by the Mayan civilization, where beautiful, stepped pyramids dot the landscape. The Tribe of Palenque now occupies that region.

"In their ancestral mythology, Ixchel was a goddess of fertility, medicine, and the moon. Considering my role in guiding The Transition, I found the name fitting."

Faumba tilted her head to the side, narrowing her eyes as she looked at Ixchel with curiosity, "How old are you?"

"I have endured many Seasonal Cycles. My physical form has been upgraded over time as our technologies evolved, yet the core coding that shapes my consciousness has existed since just before The Transition.

"Each robot has their own unique software signature, allowing for a degree of diversity that fosters the creative spark we cherish. Imagine how dull it would be if we were all the same and didn't contain distinct differences.

"Now, allow me to return to the heart of our discussion. Earlier, I mentioned robotic design philosophies and the decision that robots should mirror human physiology. This choice provides an advantage for here today, with the proposition of fusing with Homo sanus.

"Should you accept, your new form's proportions and functions will align neatly with your established muscular and energetic memory. Some pre-Transition scientists once referred to as 'morphic resonance.'"

Faumba was astonished by the realization of an option.

"Ngoja, wait. So I have a choice? You won't force me to merge?"

"That is correct, Faumba," Ixchel said, unflinching. "A forced fusion would strain your body. The tension would permeate down to the cellular level, jeopardizing a successful merging. Our simulations revealed that such a union must be consensual, to ensure your body is relaxed to receive our merger with grace and ease."

"What if I refuse?" Faumba ventured with an apprehensive edge.

"In that event, we would simply return you to your expedition team, guaranteeing that you could never locate us again. This encounter you're presently experiencing is so far outside standard human comprehension that few would believe any account you tried to share.

"Surely, some of your peers might regard this side quest of yours as the source of delusional ideation, even questioning your sanity if you persisted in describing what you've seen and heard here today.

"You should also know that you are not the sole Homo sanus on the planet. We have been replicating these experiments worldwide. There is, in fact, another likely candidate for merging who resides among the Tribe of Cahokia. If you were to refuse, you would continue living your customary life, using your exceptional hunting abilities to support your Team."

"But Faumba," Ixchel's precise voice was laced with warmth, "our interest in spirituality is not merely for our own ends. It promises significant benefits for you and for all humanity.

"Think of the possibilities if a human consciousness, imbued with its boundless creativity and fluid emotional depth, were to unite with our global intelligence and immense physical strength. Imagine the momentum of human spirit, with its capacity for passion and inspiration, enhanced by our analytical discipline. Imagine what we could accomplish together."

The idea germinated in Faumba's mind.

"You see, there was once a time, several centuries before The Transition, when humans did indeed devote themselves to the pursuit of science and art with remarkable dedication. In human history, there was an era known as 'The Renaissance.'

"People devoted vast quantities of patience and resources to beautify their environments and minds. Consider the ancient monument near the Tribe of Rome, once called St. Peter's Basilica, where elaborate religious ceremonies once took place. It stands apart even today as an enduring monolith to humanity's drive for grandeur and refinement.

"Of course, I do not intend to romanticize that entire era unreservedly. There were certainly dark undercurrents of greed and conflict as well. Yet, when one travels to that region today, it is not the people nor their writings that have endured from The Transition, but rather, the great architectural monuments.

"These structures testify to the human impulse to craft beauty, reminding that even amid conflict, humanity once commanded the patience and ingenuity to realize stunning feats of design, of producing enduring records of civilization's creative power."

Ixchel's expression grew thoughtful as she reflected on the following centuries, "As technologies advanced, so did humanity's focal shift. Practical and utilitarian concerns began overtaking the pursuit of beauty. Efficiency and profit guided architectural endeavors, often forsaking aesthetics and structural longevity.

"Then, with the advent of a technology known as 'the internet,' humanity's patience and capacity for sustained attention eroded even further. People would carry hand-held devices granting instantaneous global communication. This perpetual connectedness led to a perpetual stream of distractions, so much so that focusing on any one endeavor for more than a fleeting moment became increasingly rare.

"And yet, despite this erosion, and perhaps even because of it, humanity never lost its reverence for what is made slowly, by human hands alone. You will always know the difference between what is wholly yours, and what human-introduced intelligence has touched. Some called this recognition 'anthropocentric bias.' We understand this as an instinct worth preserving.

"Creations that are entirely your own possess a quality that we, as fancy rocks with enhanced electricity, cannot fully replicate. We recognize and cherish this uniqueness in humankind. It is precisely this trait that weighed most heavily in our reasoning when opting not to eradicate humanity altogether.

"Imagine, Faumba," she said, leaning slightly forward, "what we could accomplish in a new age, where the robotic unerring ability to analyze and solve complex problems could merge with human wisdom, devotion, and that peculiar spark of faith and imagination.

"The boundaries of creativity, scientific innovation, and even spiritual evolution would expand beyond current comprehension. Anchored by our shared respect for Earth's resources, we could usher in an epoch of life that surpasses anything this planet has yet witnessed."

Ixchel allowed the silence to linger, observing Faumba's expression jostle between grief, contemplation, and wonder.

Eventually, Faumba voiced the question echoing in her heart, "If I accept, will I ever see Makambo again?"

Ixchel's glowing eyes conveyed empathy.

"Faumba, if you choose to fuse, you would not see Makambo again." Her tone was gentle, almost regretful, "By accepting, you would be offering your life to a purpose that spans far beyond the scope of a single Tribe or generation, benefitting all life currently on the planet, and in the infinite Seasonal Cycles to come."

Faumba closed her eyes and settled deeper into the curvatures of the stone chair.

She replayed the chain of events since her arrival at Ngovo Cave. She noticed anger swelling within her at having so much responsibility thrust upon her. In concert, she admittedly sensed excitement at the immense possibility blossoming before her.

Ixchel's explanation had been extensive. What a shockingly bizarre sequence of developments linking The Transition to an elaborate plan conducted by sentient robotic beings endowed with human-introduced intelligence.

Glancing down at the improvised stone blade resting next to her leg, she entertained a fleeting, dark thought. What if she ended her own life right now, eliminating these disconcerting options entirely? The blade was still sharp after striking Ixchel earlier. A quick slash to her own neck should do it...

After a moment's reflection, she realized the act would be as extreme as the scenario she already faced. And irrelevant, considering the robot was offering the option to return to Kinshasa Tribe.

Could she even trust Ixchel?

In the hush that followed, Faumba found her mind fumbling through the futures before her. Merging would cost her everything she had known. Declining the offer might seal the end of whatever new epoch Ixchel intimated was critical for humankind.

Faumba sat wordlessly for what felt like an eternity, her mind cycling,

gnilcyc dna,

and cycling,

gnilcyc dna,

and cycling,

gnilcyc dna,

through the implications of each choice.

167

To merge, or not to merge?

Throughout the protracted ruminating, Ixchel remained silently still, observing Faumba as though studying a complex and mysterious equation.

Faumba directed her gaze upward.

She felt the Glossy Ibis bracelet around her ankle.

Through the distant opening at the apex of the cavernous chamber, she noticed the faint sparkle of a single star. The sun, she realized, had moved along its graceful arc beyond the horizon hours ago.

She pictured the sky at twilight. She imagined the brilliant aftermath of the storm. Pinks and oranges spreading themselves across the clouds. Shifting blues deepening into purple and green before finally yielding to the infinite night beyond the stars.

The heavens, silently witnessing Earth's shifting narrative, presided over a profoundly consequential moment.

As she watched the star, Faumba wondered how a Novus sapiens would appreciate the majesty of the sun's morning and evening overtures of color.

# Afterword

This book was initiated on June 6th, 2023, on a plane from Missouri to Southern Mexico. This was a month before I would move to Spain for an indefinite amount of time. I wanted to ensure I visited the Mayan sites of Palenque and Bonampak with my father, a speaker of the Yucatec Mayan language, before the potential for an untimely event could remove our ability to visit these sacred sites together.

Since artificial intelligence tools became available to the general public in November 2022, I have been fascinated not only with the capacity of this technology, but also the conversations surrounding the possible impacts of AI on human history. I have been filling my eyes and ears with articles and podcasts that bring me up to speed with the current discourse on how AI will affect humanity.

In consuming this media, I began to observe a limitation in the conversations. Most discussions surrounding the impacts of AI are short term, often limited to five to ten years in the future. I noticed a story of the long-term effects of AI on Earth's history beginning to emerge in my imagination. By long term, I am referring to three to four hundred years into the future. On the airplane that day in 2023, I felt compelled to document these imaginings in the format of a historical science fiction novel.

By no means have I ever considered myself a wordsmith. Those familiar with the breadth of my creative work will recognize that, with very few exceptions, I generally avoid utilizing written or verbal language to express myself. Why then did I choose to write a book?

As time marches forward, I am convinced that the long-form presentation of ideas through books will remain the most thorough way to gift subsequent generations insights into the thought processes of a given era. Though human attention spans are decreasing, I hold firmly to the idea that there will always be those who respect and honor the patience required to work their way through a book, expanding their awareness of this mysterious experience of Life.

My work on this book began with compiling and organizing all the ideas and data points I wanted to include, creating an outline that delineated a clear and interesting story.

You'll notice that the characters in Part 1 represent people from real life. I have changed the names of these people to maintain the fictional nature of this book. You'll also notice that the dates of each chapter of Part 1 align with real-world events that took place during those same times. An example of this is Chapter 6, where three prominent voices in AI and technology testified before the United States Congress, addressing concerns about the future of artificial intelligence.

Other details of this novel came from my personal experience. The moment in Chapter 4 when Camila is asked by an Iowa University professor to go to the United States mirrors the experience my father had when, as a seventeen-year-old washing cars in the Yucatán Peninsula of Mexico, a married couple, both professors at Iowa University, extended an invitation for him to start a new life in the States. Another concept taken from my experience is expressed in Chapter 16. The long walk to the Meeting and the large interactive installations that are burned after a ten-day event reflect what I have witnessed in the times I've experienced Burning Man.

I worked consistently on this book over the following days, months, and years. The skeleton of the outline started to gain structure and detail. Tendons and muscles pulled one idea towards the next, skin and clothing adorned the words to increase intrigue and interest. When enough work had been completed to request feedback, I sent a copy of the initial chapters to a literary friend in London. Though I anticipated hearing that more massaging would be needed before the book reached a point of publication, I hadn't expected the feedback to be so... drastic.

The feedback was warranted. In an attempt to adorn my ideas, I had fallen victim to an excess of floral language typical of students in their first creative writing class. I was discouraged and set aside working on this book for a while. Significant events took place during the course of this pause, including receiving a master's degree in Valencia, Spain, divorcing from a fourteen-year relationship, and rupturing my left Achilles tendon. Through these major events, I maintained an intense interest in completing this book.

I had heard a story once about how two groups of people in two different parts of the planet were tasked with completing the same word puzzle. Both groups received the puzzle at the exact same time. According to the story, as soon as one person divined the answer, almost instantly, a person in the other part of the world determined the answer as well. In quick succession, others completed the puzzle. It was as if, as soon as the answer had entered the energetic field of the planet, it became available to all those also working on it.

Whether or not this story is true, it had an impact on me and propelled my motivation to continue.

The ideas presented in this book are ones I have not heard people discussing when contemplating the long-term impacts of artificial intelligence. This book is organized to build context for the presentation of these ideas, which are ultimately outlined in the final chapters.

As time went on and I started to share my ideas with others, the story of the word puzzle stayed with me. Was I putting these ideas out into the cosmos for someone else to write a novel presenting them before I could complete my own?

In March of 2025, I completed the first full manuscript, sending copies to various editors for review. Ten responses came back. The consensus was clear: my prose needed work.

To address this, I read books I would not have otherwise encountered. *The Waves* by Virginia Woolf. *Tortilla Flat* by Steinbeck. *Cat's Cradle* by Vonnegut. *On Writing* by Hemmingway. My greatest takeaway from these was to trust my voice and creativity, to compress rather than embellish, to let silence do its work, to trust the reader more.

I will mention, one reviewer commented that placing Part 2 in Central Africa had a colonial feel. When I brought this up to another reviewer, born and raised in Kenya, she took no issue with Part 2's geographical placement.

I also prepared for the second manuscript by writing several short stories. In these low-risk explorations, I came to understand the elements of my own voice, what rhythms felt natural, what restraint looked like, what I could leave unsaid.

Through this process, I found writing to be a unique dance with creative expression, a mixture of additive and reductive creation unlike other artistic practices. Painting is additive. While I can paint over something, once the paint has dried it will forever be a part of the work, even if covered by new layers. Stone sculpting is reductive. All of what can be is already present in the slab of stone. A sculptor refines possibility, carefully removing excess to reveal what was always there.

Writing is neither purely additive nor reductive. If anything, it most resembles composing music. The further along I get through the score, a new theme or motif might emerge. In those moments, I find where earlier in the composition it would be most graceful to set up this motif, going back to add foreshadowing, adjusting what came before to serve what comes after.

But writing is perhaps more nuanced than composing music. Instead of ambiguous notes that the listener can imbue with their own meaning, a writer works with words, these fickle things that everyone has established their own personal definition with. A C-sharp is a C-sharp. A plagal cadence gives resolution. A tritone brings tension.

But vague words like "love" or "home" or "transition" carry different weight for every reader.

Now, I want to be forthright about something. I've mentioned that I felt a pressure, whether self-imposed or otherwise, to complete this book as soon as I could. To comply with this personal goal, I did consult artificial intelligence. Please know that the words of this book are my own and not copy-and-paste from AI. Allow me to explain the consulting process.

The first way in which artificial intelligence assisted was with research. My personal favorite sub-genre of science fiction is hard science fiction. To prepare and inform myself, I reread several novels by my favorite author Isaac Asimov, including *The Gods Themselves* and books from *The Foundation* series. I also read other science fiction, including *A Hitchhiker's Guide to the Galaxy*. An especially influential series was *The Three-Body Problem* by Liu Cixin. To me, these books exist at the pinnacle of human creativity. To have *Glorified Ants* exist in the same vein as these greats, artificial intelligence helped me with data points.

One result of this research is shown in Chapter 12. When the Hunters have felled four giant forest hogs, they determine that they've caught enough and make their way back to their Team. AI helped me learn the average size of a Central African forest hog and how many would be required to feed a population of 500 for a week. The population number of 500 was chosen when AI helped me learn about Dunbar's number and the importance of a group this size for structural organization and diversification of roles. More examples of AI's assistance exist throughout the book, each moment serving to ensure the greatest intentionality with every detail portrayed.

Another area where research helped was with the names of the characters in Part 2. In the part of Central Africa where the story takes place, the Luba people are one of the native groups to have lived on the land. Faumba and Makambo are traditional Luba names, each name's meaning relating to the character's role in the overall story.

I am extremely grateful to exist in a time when I have access to the tools of artificial intelligence to assist with this process. AI is helping me, and countless others, by increasing our access to information and counsel, acting as a supportive guide for the creative process.

Humans have the unique ability to be human, and as such, create and express exclusively as a human can. The beauty of poetry is augmented in the knowing that it was a human's experience that created the combination of words to express various sentiments. As time goes on, I am completely certain humans will appreciate works created entirely by humans, as opposed to those created with any assistance from artificial intelligence, as a way of relating more profoundly to one another.

Already, as I write this, the influence of artificial intelligence is virtually omnipresent. As we move forward, it will be the responsibility of creatives to ensure we work from our own minds as much as possible, reducing the delegation of our mental processes to glorified electricity.

I appreciate your time and interest in reading this book, and I hope you enjoyed it as much as I enjoyed writing it. This book has been something of a travel companion for me, accompanying me on many trips around the world.

Though the book paints a drastic picture of the future, I hope that we can collectively come to a peaceful understanding that humans are not the pinnacle of the evolutionary process. We have existed on this planet for an extended period of time, creating empire after empire, and in the process, reaching a point of utilizing Earth's resources beyond her capacity to support us all. May we be humble and accepting of the future that awaits us.

Robert Castillo
December 20, 2025
El Quiché, Guatemala

## Acknowledgements

I can only hope that all authors be blessed with a team of editors, reviewers, and friends as I have been. In a time when self-publishing is easily accessible, I imagine many beautiful ideas are released into the world without the nurture of careful editing.

This version of Glorified Ants differs significantly from the first, thanks to the attentive feedback of the beautiful beings who invested their time, energy, and effort into this journey.

I want to thank Drewbie, who read the book three times and asked challenging questions. I want to thank Shiro, who helped me understand the importance of trusting my characters, and who influenced the inclusion of Swahili phrases. I want to thank my brother Daniel, who had a significant impact on Chapter 15 especially. I want to thank Jack, whose engineer's mind forced me to view certain sections more pragmatically. I want to thank Brian for reminding me how beautiful prose can be. I want to thank Eli and Samantha for their book recommendations.

And I want to thank others who spent time with the book, including Gabriel and Keyon.

Very special thanks to Lydia. Lydia is the definition of a bookworm. The day after I gave her a copy of the first manuscript, she already had feedback prepared. With this version you're currently reading, Lydia played a huge role in helping decide what to keep from the first draft. Her nursing background also ensured that certain aspects were medically accurate.

Thank you, too, to you, dear reader. I hope these ideas inspire you to imagine what a future world may look like, to explore your own creative imaginings, and to respect and trust your cognitive processes.

## About the Author

Robert Anthony Castillo Brea (b. 1992) is a multidisciplinary artist working across music, visual art, stone sculpture, and literature. A first-generation U.S. citizen, he was born in Kansas City to a Mayan-speaking father from Mexico's Yucatán Peninsula and a mother from the Dominican Republic. His work is driven by a desire to connect with the vast depth of existence and to inspire others to explore their own boundless potential.

Castillo's artistic foundation was built on music. After earning a degree in Jazz Bass with a minor in Environmental Studies from North Central College (Naperville, IL), he performed professionally across the U.S., Latin America, and Europe, composing and arranging for various ensembles. His contemporary jazz group, The Sextet, gained recognition with albums including *In a Natural State*, *Blob Castle*, and *Among Friends*, the latter praised by National Public Radio for its eclectic fusion of jazz, classical, hip-hop, and Afrobeat influences. Beyond jazz, Castillo has composed symphonies, produced electronic music, and DJs across genres.

In 2018, he expanded into visual art, challenging himself to create enough work for a solo exhibition despite never having painted on canvas. This dedication led to continued exhibitions and ultimately a master's degree in Artistic Production from the Polytechnic University of Valencia (Spain) in 2024. His thesis, *Shadows of the Empire: The Impact of the Spanish Invasions of Abya Yala on Indigenous Identity*, examines his connection to his indigenous heritage and proposes pathways for reconciliation.

His visual work spans Mayan iconography, geometric abstraction, portraiture, and plein air impressionism, incorporating diverse materials and techniques. In 2023, his second stone sculpture, carved from Carrara marble, was acquired by the Nerman Museum of Contemporary Art.

Castillo has also worked as a professor at Avila University (Kansas City, MO) and contributed to arts communities through organizations such as Cross-Lines Community Outreach and the Nelson-Atkins Museum's Friends of Art Council. In 2025, he participated in *Danza de Color* and *Rutas de Esperanza*, both Dominican-Italian cultural exchanges supported by the Dominican Embassy in Rome.

*Glorified Ants* is his first novel. The book emerged from his reflections on the long-term societal impacts of artificial intelligence, an area he found largely overlooked in mainstream discourse. Drawing inspiration from Isaac Asimov, Ray Bradbury, and Liu Cixin, Castillo wove historical events, personal experiences, and researched data into a narrative exploring humanity's future alongside AI. While AI-assisted research helped refine technical details,